'Miss Carrie D... we meet again,'

Carrie hadn't a clue ...
me,' she said in a polite but firm tone, 'but actually I'm wondering what you're doing here.'

'It's you who should forgive me.' He held out his hand to her. 'Here I am in your home and I haven't even introduced myself. I'm Leone,' he told her. 'Leone Montecrespi.'

He held her eyes and smiled. 'We have unfinished business.'

'I wasn't aware that you and I had any business to finish.'

'Perhaps not, strictly speaking, *business*.'

Count Leone Alberto Cosimo George di Montecrespi, the heir to the throne of San Rinaldo, simply smiled at her reaction. I'm going to enjoy this, he was thinking. This one's definitely no pushover. It would make a pleasant change from the easy victories he was used to.

Dear Reader,

Welcome to Royal Affair! By appointment to her loyal readers, Stephanie Howard has created a blue-blooded trilogy of Romeos, rebels and royalty. It follows the fortunes of the San Rinaldo royal family: Damiano, the Duke of San Rinaldo, his brother, Count Leone, and their sister, Lady Caterina. Together the three of them are dedicated to their country, people and family. But it takes only one thing to turn their perfectly ordered lives upside down: love!

COUNT LEONE MONTECRESPI, the younger brother of the ruling Duke, was a habitual heartbreaker. A playboy of the old school: love them, leave them and on no account marry them. But would small-town American girl Carrie Dunn be the one to finally get him up the aisle?

LADY CATERINA MONTECRESPI, Leone and Damiano's baby sister, had sworn off men since her last disastrous encounter with the opposite sex. And Matthew Allenby was hardly the man to change her mind. As far as Caterina was concerned, he was a crook and a charlatan. Unfortunately he was also proving irresistible!

The DUKE OF SAN RINALDO, DAMIANO MONTECRESPI, had married Sofia to secure his dukedom and produce an heir. But duty for Sofia was a cold bed partner–she wanted Damiano to love her as much as he did their baby son, Alessandro. Was a happy ending to their fairy-tale romance too much to ask for?

Each of these books contains its own stand-alone romance as well as making up a great trilogy. Follow Leone and Carrie's tale in THE COLORADO COUNTESS. In THE LADY'S MAN it's the turn of Caterina and Matthew. And finally THE DUKE'S WIFE features Sofia and Damiano's story–not forgetting little baby Alessandro!

With three royal weddings and a baby, this is one series you don't want to miss!

Happy reading!

The Editor

THE COLORADO COUNTESS

BY
STEPHANIE HOWARD

MILLS & BOON

*MILLS & BOON and the Rose Device
are trademarks of the publisher.
Harlequin Mills & Boon Limited,
Eton House, 18-24 Paradise Road, Richmond, Surrey TW9 1SR*

© Stephanie Howard 1996

ISBN 0 263 79475 X

*Set in Times Roman 10½ on 12 pt.
01-9605-50540 C1*

Made and printed in Great Britain

Stephanie Howard was born and brought up in Dundee in Scotland, and educated at the London School of Economics. For ten years she worked as a journalist in London on a variety of women's magazines, among them *Woman's Own*, and was latterly editor of the now defunct *Honey*. She has spent many years living and working abroad—in Italy, Malaysia, the Philippines and in the Middle East.

Recent titles by the same author:

COME BACK FOREVER
THE BEST FOR LAST
THE MAN WHO BROKE HEARTS

THE MONTECRESPI ROYAL FAMILY TREE

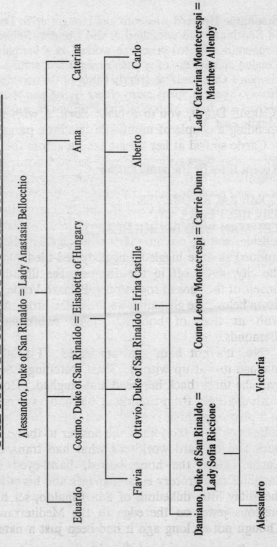

Alessandro, Duke of San Rinaldo = Lady Anastasia Bellocchio

Cosimo, Duke of San Rinaldo = Elisabetta of Hungary

Eduardo

Anna

Caterina

Ottavio, Duke of San Rinaldo = Irina Castille

Flavia

Alberto

Carlo

Count Leone Montecrespi = Carrie Dunn

Lady Caterina Montecrespi = Matthew Allenby

Damiano, Duke of San Rinaldo = Lady Sofia Riccione

Alessandro

Victoria

CHAPTER ONE

'CARRIE DUNN, you're a lucky devil. I wish *I* was spending a couple of months in this little paradise!'

Carrie smiled at her friend Louise across the table where they were sitting, right at the very front of the magnificent terrace of the ultra-chic restaurant where they had come for dinner. Then she turned to cast a glance at the magical view spread out before them— a shimmer of lights that seemed to tumble down the hillside, setting out in sharp relief against the star-studded sky the higgledy-piggledy red-tiled roofs of the city, with, off in the distance, the illuminated turrets of the ancient rosy-stoned Palazzo Verde, and, down below, the glistening waters of the little marina, with its fleet of bobbing yachts twinkling like diamonds.

'No, it's not bad,' she consented. 'I think I'll manage to put up with it.' Then, catching Louise's eye, she threw back her head and laughed. 'How on earth did a girl from Boulder, Colorado, ever end up in a place like this?'

Both girls, in fact, knew the answer to that one. A bucketful of hard work was what had transported Carrie Dunn, the honey-haired, hazel-eyed elder daughter of a grocery store manager and his wife, to the glitzy little dukedom of San Rinaldo, set like a precious jewel on the edge of the Mediterranean. Though not so long ago it had been just a name to

7

her, a place she'd simply read about in glossy magazines, famous for its wines and its wonderful porcelain, for the rich and famous who came here on holiday and, last but not least, for its colourful ruling family.

For the Montecrespis, the royal residents of the ancient Palazzo Verde—the Duke, Damiano, and his wife, his playboy brother, Count Leone, and their younger sister, Lady Caterina—had a knack of making newspaper headlines. Especially Count Leone, who went through more women than a brigade of Guards. Even Carrie, who didn't much interest herself with such things, had heard a fair bit about the dashing count and his exploits.

But all the gossip and glamour associated with San Rinaldo were not what had brought Carrie to the sun-drenched little dukedom. And she assured her friend now, pulling a face as she did so, 'Don't worry, I promise I won't let it go to my head. You can go back to New York tomorrow with no worries on that score. The only reason I'm here is to work.'

'Oh, I know it won't go to your head,' Louise threw her a frank look. 'You're not the type.' For she knew Carrie well. Then she glanced round her and laughed. 'But how can you even *think* of work in a place like this?'

Carrie was about to answer good-humouredly that she always thought of work, but at that moment she was distracted by the sound of raised voices coming from the end of the busy, table-packed terrace. As she turned curiously to look, a frowning waiter was hurrying towards them.

He stopped before their table, wringing his hands as he addressed Carrie.

'Apologies, *signorina*, but there's been a most regrettable error. This table you're sitting at...you should never have been given it. It was already booked, you see...' He glanced wretchedly across his shoulder at the noisy group of young people at the end of the terrace. 'Your table and the one next to it... These people booked them some time ago. I really do apologise, but I'm going to have to move you to another table...'

'And what if we don't want to move?'

It wasn't like Carrie to be awkward, but on this occasion she felt she was more than justified.

'My friend and I are halfway through our meal,' she protested. 'I'm afraid it really would be most inconvenient.'

And besides, she was thinking, it rather stuck in her throat to be moved for the convenience of the group of young people in question, who more than likely hadn't booked the table at all. They were obviously celebrities. They positively oozed self-importance. Her skin prickled as one of them called out now, in English, 'Come on, waiter! What are we waiting for? Tell them they can go and sit at the back.'

What bad-mannered hooligans! Carrie glared in their direction. 'Maybe *they* should go and sit at the back,' she muttered.

But Louise was trying to persuade her. 'Let's just move,' she was urging. 'We've almost finished anyway and I'd rather avoid the hassle.'

Carrie could feel herself weakening. She knew how Louise hated scenes, and this evening was supposed to be a special treat for her—just to thank her for dropping by on her way back to the States after a business trip to Rome. So, reluctantly, she agreed. 'Ok,' she told the waiter—though she was thinking as they were moved to a half-hidden table at the back, I'll never set foot in this restaurant again!

It was about twenty minutes later, after the two girls had had coffee and Louise had disappeared off to powder her nose, that Carrie decided to call for the bill. And it was as she was signalling to the waiter that, from the corner of her eye, she became aware of a tall figure at the table she had so recently vacated rising to his feet and coming across the terrace. But she did not turn to look at him. She would not honour him with a glance. Pompous, self-important swine, she was thinking.

But then, a moment later, to her total astonishment, she was aware that he had come to stand at her elbow. Then a voice said, 'Signorina, may I have a word with you?'

Something had jolted inside Carrie even before she looked up. There was something in the voice, with its soft, smoky accent, that sent a shiver of expectation rippling down her spine. Feeling somewhat taken aback at herself, she slowly raised her eyes.

And that was when her heart did a somersault in her chest.

His face was in shadow, so she couldn't see him clearly—for the lighting here at the back of the terrace was far from bright. But, shadow or not, his effect on her was electric. What a perfectly spectacular-looking guy!

And there was something else as well. Didn't she know him from somewhere? For there was something a little familiar about the high-cheekboned face, with its amused, sensuous mouth and broad, intelligent brow, the dark-as-midnight eyes that seemed to smoulder with secrets and the curling black hair that fell to just below his ears. She couldn't think where, but she'd seen him somewhere before.

All this went through Carrie's head as she hurriedly pulled herself together and responded in a tone that impressed even her with its perfect calmness. 'A word?' What could he possibly want to have a word with her about?

The stranger answered that question immediately. 'I wish to apologise,' he said.

'Apologise?' Carrie blinked at him.

'For the unfortunate business concerning your table.'

Ah, the table. She had quite forgotten about the table, bowled over as she had been by the sheer seductive power of him. But, now that he had reminded her, she felt her attitude abruptly change. How foolish of her to be so easily seduced by a handsome face! He was one of the band of hooligans who had pinched her table!

She looked back at him, quite recovered, a distinct edge to her voice now. 'I would have thought,' she pointed out, 'that it's a little late for that.'

'I agree. It is. But I wanted to apologise, anyway.'

As he spoke, the dark eyes travelled quite openly over her, taking in her slender, feminine figure, currently dressed in a cream top and trousers that showed off the light tan she'd acquired in the few days she'd been here, skimming her heart-shaped face in its frame of cropped blonde hair, pausing to admire the wide hazel eyes, the tip-tilted nose and the soft-lipped mouth—though the latter, at this moment, was set in a disapproving line.

How dare he eye me like that? Carrie was thinking to herself irritably, though his gaze was so direct, his expression so open that it was really a little hard to take offence. And, if she was strictly honest with herself, she would have to admit that he was studying her no more carefully than she was secretly studying him.

He was tall, over six feet, in his early thirties, she guessed, with the lean and supple build of an athlete. Beneath the blue linen jacket his shoulders were broad and muscular, and there was something about the way he stood, on those long legs in their dark blue trousers, that suggested a powerful, restless energy. He really was rather seriously sexy.

No, he wasn't, she contradicted herself. He was one of those awful hooligans. Some minor celebrity she couldn't quite put a name to who thought he had the right to behave with total arrogance and who was simply amusing himself by coming over to apologise. No doubt she was supposed to feel deeply privileged and grateful.

Carrie narrowed her eyes as he continued to look at her with that half-amused, half-scrutinising gaze. 'Well, you've apologised now,' she pointed out in a clipped tone, 'so I guess you can go back and rejoin your friends.'

'You're still angry, I see?' One dark eyebrow lifted. 'Well, I can't really blame you. This is a far inferior table. I guess, if I were in your shoes, I'd be pretty angry too.'

That was patronising. What would he know about being in her shoes? Celebrities like him, whoever he was, were unlikely ever to encounter such disagreeable situations. Instead, they went about creating them for ordinary mortals like her.

She continued to squint at him, trying to put a name to his face. Was he a singer? An actor? Maybe he was in the theatre? For there was definitely something rather classy about him.

But, classy or not, he was making her bristle. She informed him in a cutting tone, 'I can assure you, if it had been up to me, I'd have refused point-blank to move to this table. But I'm here with a friend and she didn't want a fuss. That's the only reason you and your friends got our table.'

'I see.' He smiled. Her disapproval merely amused him, as did her claim that she would have stood up to him. 'You believe in fighting for your rights, I see? That's most commendable.'

'And very necessary, I'd say, when there are so many people . . .' As she said it she glanced pointedly across the terrace at his friends. 'So many people about with such little regard for the rights of others.'

Again the dark eyebrows rose and again he smiled at her, and there was something so bright and so beguiling about that smile that Carrie very nearly forgot herself and smiled right back at him. But she resisted and continued to scowl at him as he responded, 'I see you consider that my friends need teaching some manners. Well, perhaps you have a point. And that's why I'm here to apologise.'

'Well, that's very nice of you.' Carrie's tone was barbed with sarcasm. 'But, as I said, it's a little late in the day for apologies. And an apology doesn't change the fact that our dinner was spoiled.'

The stranger continued to watch her with that smouldering dark gaze he had that, though she was trying hard to fight it, was sending pins and needles through her. And Carrie was annoyed at herself, for it was perfectly obvious that he was an expert at reducing women to quivering lumps of jelly. He had that air of a seducer. He would know women well. How to draw them to him and how to please him. From the top of his beautiful head to the tips of his elegant fingertips, one could sense he was something of an expert in that field.

Carrie was considering this judgement and deciding it was another reason to dislike him when he surprised her by asking, 'Which part of America are you from? I can't quite manage to pin down your accent.'

Carrie had not expected this—that the conversation would turn personal. 'Colorado,' she said curtly, deliberately not elaborating that for the past three years she'd lived and worked in New York and that there was a touch of the Big Apple in her accent as well. If he was trying to hit on her, he'd find he'd fallen on stony ground!

And then, because she was sure it would almost certainly annoy him, for nothing annoyed a minor celebrity more than not being recognised, she added, regarding him levelly, her tone indicating that her interest was minimal, 'And what about you? Where do you come from?'

He held her gaze for a moment, a smile flitting across his eyes. 'Me? Oh, I'm just a local,' he responded. Then, while she digested this, wondering if it was true, for San Rinaldo was not exactly famous for its showbiz celebrities, he continued, 'Colorado? That's a part of the States I've never visited. But I understand from friends who've been there that it's extremely beautiful.'

'Yes, it is.' She eyed him. More condescension, she was thinking. He would have dredged up some friends who'd told him it was beautiful if she'd told him she came from a hole in the ground.

'You're a visitor here?'

'Sort of,' she answered unhelpfully. Was he trying to win her round now by feigning interest in her humble life?

She peered at him. If only she could think who he was. It was on the tip of her brain. If only she could see him better. If only his features weren't in shadow all the time.

' "Sort of". And what does that mean?' He continued to watch her, and she could see that amused smile hovering round his lips. 'Are you here on holiday? Are you a tourist?'

'Not exactly.'

'Not exactly?' He waited for her to elaborate. He was totally unfazed by her hostile lack of co-operation.

Carrie took a deep breath. She might as well tell him, then she could ask him the same question and finally find out who he was.

'I happen to be here for reasons of work,' she told him.

He feigned interest. 'And what kind of work is that?'

'I'm putting together a book.'

'A book? That sounds fascinating. May I enquire what kind of book?'

'A book on Castello porcelain.' Then she added unnecessarily, for if he really was a local he would surely already know, 'It's a locally made porcelain that's famous throughout the world. Over the centuries it's graced the tables of every royal family in Europe, not to mention the table at the White House also.'

He was smiling. 'Ah, so you are capable of stringing more than one sentence together. I was beginning to think you had a serious communication problem.'

Very amusing. But Carrie did not smile back. She'd already been thinking she'd been just a little too forthcoming. It was her enthusiasm for the project that had momentarily got the better of her, for this book she was putting together on Castello porcelain—*literally* putting together, for she was both writing it and doing the photographs!—was undoubtedly one of the most exciting projects she'd ever worked on. Ever since her New York editor had first OK'd the idea two months ago she had barely been able to think of anything else. And she loved talking about it to anyone who would listen!

But she hadn't intended to confide her passion to this arrogant dark stranger, who now knew a little too much about her for her liking—especially since she still knew nothing about him!

And it was time to put that right. She regarded him boldly. 'But enough about me. Tell me something about you. For example, what do you do for a living?'

'Me?'

He continued to smile at her and did not answer immediately, almost as though he was pondering how to respond. Perhaps he was astonished that she didn't know. Or insulted—though he did not look it. Rather, he looked intrigued, Carrie decided as she waited, wondering what had prompted this unlikely display of reticence.

'Now it looks as though *you're* the one with the communication problem,' she pointed out.

He laughed then. '*Touché*!' Then he smiled. 'Well, since you ask . . .'

But he never finished the sentence, for at that very moment a man in a dark suit suddenly appeared at his elbow, murmuring something in Italian that Carrie couldn't understand. Damn! she was thinking as her still unidentified stranger, with a polite nod in her direction, turned away to reply to him. Wouldn't you just believe it? Talk about bad timing!

'I'm afraid I have to go.' He was turning back to look at her. 'It would appear my presence is required elsewhere.'

Then, surprising her, he held out his hand for a brief handshake. 'It's been most interesting meeting you. And again, let me offer you my apologies. I hope your bad experience this evening won't spoil your stay here.'

And, before she had time to do more than mumble, 'I'm sure it won't,' he was turning sharply on his heel and disappearing into the interior part of the restaurant.

Not, Carrie thought wryly as she watched his departure, that she would have been capable of saying much more anyway. That brief handshake had quite literally galvanised her for a moment. The touch of his skin had seemed to scorch against her. In those brief seconds of contact she'd been aware of a raw vitality that had sent shock waves down to the soles of her feet.

Phew! Whoever he was, this guy was pure dynamite!

She was rather glad to be brought back to earth as the waiter appeared at the next table and she suddenly remembered that he still hadn't brought her the bill. She waved to catch his attention. 'My bill, please,' she called, but he was already coming over.

'*Signorina*,' he smiled. 'There is no bill.' He shrugged an expressive shrug. 'It has already been paid.'

'Paid?'

'Yes, *signorina*.'

'By whom has it been paid?' Though Carrie had a sneaking suspicion that she already knew the answer.

The waiter made a gesture as though reluctant to divulge this information. Then he murmured conspiratorially, confirming her suspicion, 'By the gentleman you were just speaking to a moment ago.'

'But he had no right to do that!' Carrie was already rising to her feet indignantly. 'I'm perfectly capable of paying my own bills!'

And before the waiter could stop her, if indeed he even thought of trying, she was grabbing her bag and

steaming across the terrace in the direction her mis-
guided benefactor had taken. Who the devil did he
think he was?

There was no sign of him in the inner restaurant,
but he couldn't have gone far. Carrie headed for the
door that led to the foyer at the front. And as she
pushed the door open she beamed in triumph to
herself. He hadn't escaped her, after all. She'd arrived just in the nick of time!

He was standing by the open door, just about to
step out into the street, his back towards her so he
couldn't see her. And on the pavement ahead of him
was the man in the dark suit who was now holding
open the door of a black limousine which was conveniently parked just a couple of steps away.

Nice, Carrie thought scathingly as she stepped
boldly towards her quarry. No wonder he thinks he
can behave all high and mighty if this is the way he
gets treated all the time!

The thought fired up her anger. In a tight voice,
she called out to him, 'Just a minute, if you don't
mind! I'm afraid I've got a bone to pick with you!'
She continued to hurry up to him. 'About that high-
handed gesture of yours . . . that high-handed gesture
of paying my bill for me . . .'

Then her voice trailed off. He had turned round to
look at her. And, suddenly, Carrie was dying a
thousand deaths all in one go. For now, in the much
brighter light of the foyer, she had instantly recognised who he was.

How could I have been so stupid? she berated
herself sickly, wishing she could just melt into the
carpet and disappear. How could I have been so dim

as not to recognise him instantly? And much worse, how could I have been so gross as to speak to him the way I just did?

Her heart had stopped inside her, her flesh turned to stone. Me and my big mouth. Now I'm really going to be in trouble! she thought.

But if she was, it was not just yet.

He threw her a look she could not decipher. Then with a small lift of the eyebrow he told her, 'I'm sorry, I'm in a hurry. Some other time, perhaps. I can't stop now.'

Then he was turning away, sweeping across the pavement and climbing into the back of the black limousine. And Carrie was still standing there, speechlessly staring at it, when a moment later it purred away.

'Ah, there you are! The waiter said you'd left. I'm sorry I took such ages. I met someone in the john.'

Carrie turned woodenly to look at Louise who had just appeared at her elbow. Her brain was still spinning inside her head like a top.

'I met this woman who's here on holiday and— would you believe it?—she lives just two blocks away from me in Queen's! Can you imagine? What a co-incidence! Anyway, we got talking, and— Hey, Carrie, are you all right?' Louise paused and peered into the face of her friend who hadn't heard a single word she'd been saying. 'You look a bit strange. Has something happened?'

'I'm not sure what's happened. I think I'm going mad.' Carrie gave herself a shake and smiled a wry smile at her friend. 'I've just had a most fascinating encounter myself. And I'm afraid I've really put my foot in it.

'I thought I was speaking to just any old Prince Charming. But I wasn't. For once, I was speaking to the real thing.' She sighed and turned to the open door through which the dark stranger had disappeared. 'I'm afraid I've just made a terrible *faux pas*. I've just insulted Count Leone, the heir to the throne.'

'Here you are, sir. These are the papers I mentioned. The Duke would be grateful if you would sign them at your earliest convenience.'

'Just leave them on the table, Pierre.' Leone turned to glance at his private secretary who had appeared with the usual daily batch of papers to be dealt with. 'I'll take a look at them while I'm having breakfast,' he told him. 'You can pick them up in about half an hour.'

'Certainly, sir.' Pierre nodded deferentially. 'Will there be anything else for the moment?'

'Not for the moment, thanks.' Then, as the other man started to go, he called after him, 'Oh, by the way, congratulations. I hear you've finally fixed the big day. Well, it's about time the lovely Margherita made an honest man of you, I'd say.'

Pierre smiled a pleased smile. 'Thank you, sir,' he responded. 'We both hope you'll honour us with your presence at the wedding.'

'Wouldn't miss it for the world. You know how I love weddings.' Leone laughed. 'Just as long as they're not mine, of course.'

It was just after seven-thirty at the Palazzo Verde, and Count Leone Alberto Cosimo George di

Montecrespi, brother of the ruling Duke and heir to the throne of San Rinaldo, currently dressed in a red silk dressing gown, was in his private apartments getting ready for the day.

And it would be a full day as usual, he was thinking as he drank his coffee. Thank heavens he could rely on Pierre to organise everything.

At that moment his valet appeared from the adjoining dressing room where he'd been laying out Leone's clothes for the day.

Leone glanced at him. 'Thanks, Silvestro,' he told him. Then he enquired good-humouredly, 'I suppose you've heard Pierre's news? You know about the imminent betrothal?'

'Yes, sir. I heard about it. And very pleased I was too.'

Leone smiled at the young man. 'Another romantic, I see. No doubt you'll shortly be following in his footsteps?'

'I sincerely hope so, sir. As soon as Anna's twenty-one—and that's only eighteen months away.'

Leone shook his head at him. 'You're all mad, if you ask me. With so many beautiful, available women in the world, why any man under forty would want to get married is an absolute, total mystery to me.' And, with a smile, he turned his attention back to the pile of papers.

Not that his attention was entirely on what he was doing as he flicked his way rapidly through the papers, scanning a few lines here and there, scribbling his signature where it was required. For there was a niggling little diversion that had been occupying his thoughts with a fair degree of frequency since yesterday evening. He'd tried to dismiss it from his mind, but it refused to be dismissed, and he was rapidly coming to the conclusion that he'd have to do something about it.

Well, why not? he decided. And he smiled at the prospect. A beautiful girl is a beautiful girl, no matter how stroppy she is!

When Pierre returned, he had finished signing the papers. He handed them over. 'These all seem to be in order.' Then, sitting back in his seat and draining his coffee-cup, he added, 'I want you to track down someone for me. A girl. An American. I don't know her name, but she's blonde, mid-twenties and extremely beautiful and she's putting together a book, apparently, on Castello porcelain. Find out who she is and where she's staying and anything else you can about her.'

'Is this an urgent matter, sir?' His secretary's expression had never altered, though a look of fond amusement had briefly crossed his face. This wasn't the first time he'd been given such a task.

'Yes, it is urgent, Pierre.' Leone laid down his coffee-cup and there was a distinctly determined look in his eyes. 'This young lady and I have unfinished business.'

CHAPTER TWO

THE house Carrie had rented for her stay in San Rinaldo was about five miles out of Rino, the capital of the little dukedom, up a sun-dappled, twisting, tree-lined road with a spectacular view out over the city.

To be more accurate, she'd rented only part of the house—a marvellous red-tiled eighteenth-century villa. She'd taken the top floor, which was bright and spacious, with its own front door and huge balconies at the front and back. And she was out on the front balcony now, basking in the July sunshine, with a bowl of peaches at her elbow and a notepad on her knee as she sat in one of the comfy cane chairs and worked out her itinerary for the coming week. And it promised to be a busy one, with lots of meetings and appointments. To her enormous satisfaction, though she'd been here less than a week, work was already getting under way.

But that was Carrie's way. When it came to matters of work, she liked to dive straight in and get on with the job. And that was why, in the space of just three years, she'd gained a reputation for being a top-rank professional.

It was hard to believe, but it really was just three years ago that she had arrived in New York fresh from college with no experience at all of the publishing world, just a lot of ambition and a fistful of good ideas. Plus an infinite supply of determination, of course. For she'd quickly lost count of the publishing-house doors she'd had to knock on before one finally took her on to do a book on Colorado gold— for her native state was once prospector country— and since the success of that book her career had never looked back.

There had followed a book on Amerindian art, then one on New York's Guggenheim Museum, as well as the steady stream of magazine articles she wrote. But this latest project, the book on Castello porcelain that she had come to San Rinaldo to work on, promised to be the most ambitious so far. This one was going to be really special.

She sat back in her chair now with a smile on her face and gazed for a moment at the peaceful panorama of cypress-clad hills and green-shuttered villas. What a wonderful place. She was going to adore the next three months here. With a sigh of contentment, she reached for a peach.

At that moment there was the sound of a car down below, turning into the gravel driveway of the villa. Carrie munched on her peach, which was sweet and delicious, and turned her attention back to her scribblings. It must be someone for her landlady, a widow who lived below. Signora Rossi frequently had visitors.

She heard a car door slam, then male footsteps crossing the driveway, past the stone steps that led to her balcony. Though she was barely paying attention. She was carefully studying her itinerary, wondering if she hadn't maybe over-committed herself tomorrow. And she didn't bother to glance up when, a moment or two later, there was the sound of voices down below her balcony—Signora Rossi and her visitor talking in

Italian. So she was totally taken by surprise when suddenly her landlady called out, 'Signorina Carrie! There's someone to see you!'

How odd. Frowning a little, Carrie laid down her notepad, got to her feet and stepped to the edge of the balcony. Who on earth could it possibly be? She didn't know anyone who was likely to come visiting.

She leaned over the balcony. 'Thank you, Signora Rossi.'

But then she paused. Where was her visitor? And what manner of lightning bolt had apparently struck her landlady? For the poor woman's eyes were fixed, saucer-sized in their amazement, on the narrow stone stairway that led to Carrie's veranda.

Curious, Carrie turned to follow the stupefied gaze. Then she blinked, her own eyes transforming into saucers of amazement. For ascending the stone stairway was no less a personage than Count Leone Alberto Cosimo George di Montecrespi, the heir to the throne of San Rinaldo, whom she had so grievously insulted just two days ago.

She felt herself turn pale. Oh, dear heavens! she was thinking. He's come personally to throw me out of the country!

He had reached the top of the stairs, where he paused now to address her. 'Miss Carrie Dunn from Colorado, we meet again,' he smiled. Then he paused and regarded her pale, fixed face. 'I hope I haven't caught you at an inconvenient moment?'

'Not at all. Of course not.'

Carrie hadn't a clue what to say or do. So she just stood there, utterly immobile, feeling totally foolish in her skimpy pink shorts and strappy T-shirt, wishing that, at least, she were more soberly dressed. Though he was pretty informally attired too, in a pair of cream cotton trousers, an open-neck blue shirt and light canvas shoes. Nevertheless, he was still a count, the brother of the ruler of San Rinaldo and a member of one of the oldest noble families in Europe. Her brain was churning in confusion. Ought she to curtsy to him, or what?

Leone, for his part, was feeling a touch bemused too. She was even lovelier than he had remembered. Slender and graceful, with a natural, unadorned beauty, and a perfectly spectacular pair of legs. He looked into her face with its wide hazel eyes, gentle mouth and tip-tilted nose and was suddenly struck by the strong resemblance she bore to one of the angels in the painted frieze of the family chapel.

That surprising thought made him smile. That angel had always been his favourite.

But his task at the moment was to put this poor angel at her ease. She was standing there, quite rigid, clutching a half-eaten peach and looking as though she believed he was about to devour her.

He glanced around him. 'What a lovely place. That's a pretty spectacular view you've got.'

'Yes, it is pretty spectacular.'

Carrie managed to answer him, though her voice sounded strange, as though it belonged to someone else. What was he doing here? she kept asking herself frantically, over and over. It was bizarre. She couldn't begin to imagine what he might want of her. Though one part of her, in spite of her quite genuine anxiety, felt like laughing out loud at the situation. If only her family, or friend Louise, could see her now, standing here hobnobbing with the heir to the San Rinaldo throne!

Well, not exactly hobnobbing! That thought brought her up sharply. If her family could see her now, they'd think she was a proper wimp! She straightened her spine carefully and lifted up her chin and, suddenly realising she was still clutching her half-eaten peach, laid it carefully on the little table behind her. Then, taking a deep breath and feeling much more in control now, she forced herself to look her visitor straight in the eye.

'Forgive me,' she said in a polite but firm tone, 'but actually I'm wondering what you're doing here.' Then, a little amazed but thoroughly pleased with herself for taking this initiative, she held her breath and waited for his answer.

Leone looked at her and smiled. Good for her, he was thinking. He knew from their last confrontation that she didn't lack spirit, but last time she hadn't been aware of who he was. This time she clearly was and he'd wondered if her attitude might alter. That little demonstration that it hadn't made her even more interesting.

'Actually, it's you who should forgive me.' He held out his hand to her. 'Here I am in your home and I haven't even introduced myself. I'm Leone,' he told her. 'Leone Montecrespi.'

Carrie continued to look at him with steady hazel eyes. 'Yes, I know who you are.' Reluctantly, she took his hand, for she remembered all too vividly the effect of his handshake at the restaurant.

And it happened again, that jolt of sensation, that sense that suddenly her flesh was burning. Though she managed to control her reaction this time as she added, 'Last time we met, I confess, I didn't recognise you.' She dropped her hand away, ignoring the fierce tingling. 'The light in the restaurant wasn't very good.'

Carrie wondered as she said it if that confession was good enough. Perhaps he would expect her to apologise more profusely, possibly even grovel a bit? But grovelling was out. She just wasn't a groveller. And anyway, she reflected, she'd been perfectly entitled to make the comments she'd made the other night at the restaurant. He and his friends had behaved in a thoroughly arrogant manner.

'Yes, the light was rather poor.' Leone's reaction was simply to smile. Then he let his eyes drift over her for a moment. 'Now that I can see you properly I realise you're twice as beautiful as I'd thought.'

'Really?' Carrie's tone was flat and dismissive. Flattery will get you nowhere, it candidly told him. Whatever he'd come for, he wouldn't butter her up that way—though privately she had to confess that she'd been having similar thoughts about him!

In the warm light of day he looked even more gorgeous, and he was immeasurably more attractive, though she would hardly have thought this possible, than in the photographs she had seen of him in various glossy magazines.

There was a wonderful raw vitality to him that, along with the wild black hair and the eyes that she could see now were the pefect blue of lapis lazuli, projected an aura of shimmering excitement. She felt a rush inside her and quickly suppressed it.

She said, turning away, waving at the group of cane chairs behind her, 'Would you care to take a seat?'

Beware, she was thinking as a bell rang in her head. It had struck her in the restaurant that he was clearly a bit of a Romeo, but now that she knew who he was she knew also that she'd been right.

In those photographs one saw of him in the glossy magazines he was invariably accompanied by some pouting bimbette—always head-turningly beautiful and never the same one twice. And, though it seemed unlikely—what would he see in a girl like her who, after all, was definitely no bimbette, a very far cry from the type he went for?—it was possible that he had come here with seduction on his mind.

She darted a glance into the smoky blue eyes. Who could tell? Maybe His Highness felt like a change. Maybe he had grown a little bored with his habitual diet and fancied a working American girl instead. Perhaps he had come here to invite her to share the royal bed.

At that thought, to Carrie's dismay, she felt another rush inside her, as though all her insides had turned to liquid honey. Shame on you, she told herself, and quickly suppressed it. No matter how gorgeous he was, he would have no luck with her. She wasn't here to provide entertainment for any playboy count!

He was accepting her invitation and crossing the veranda to seat himself in the cane chair where she had been sitting earlier, the one next to the little table with the bowl of peaches. He stretched out his long legs. 'You asked what I'm doing here.' Then he held her eyes and smiled. 'We have unfinished business.'

'Unfinished business?'

What on earth did he mean by that? Carrie crossed to seat herself on one of the chairs opposite him, careful to arrange her legs at a safe distance from his, her feet crossed neatly at the ankles.

She looked him straight in the eye and raised one questioning eyebrow. 'I wasn't aware that you and I had any business to finish.'

'Perhaps not, strictly speaking, *business*.' He simply smiled at her reaction. I'm going to enjoy this, he was thinking. This one's definitely no pushover. It would make a pleasant change from the easy victories he was used to.

He stretched his legs a little further and leaned back in his seat and watched her. 'The other evening, you may remember, as I was leaving the restaurant, you came running after me, rather anxious to tell me something. I couldn't stop at the time, but perhaps you'd like to tell me about it now?'

'Is that why you've come here?' Carrie frowned as she looked back at him. 'Just to find out why I came running after you?'

She wasn't sure if she believed him. At the time, she'd been quite certain that he'd heard perfectly well her angry protests about the bill.

But perhaps not, after all, and perhaps that really was why he'd come—to find out what she'd been saying and, possibly, to chastise her for her rudeness. Perhaps she'd been totally wrong about the seduction bit. Oh, well, she thought, thank heavens for that.

Another thought struck her. He must have gone to a fair bit of trouble in order to track her down like this. She delivered him a dry look. 'How extraordinarily fastidious of you.'

'I'm an extraordinarily fastidious chap.' He smiled a lazy smile and cast a glance at the bowl of peaches at his elbow. 'What lovely-looking peaches. Do you mind if I have one?'

Then, as she nodded and said, 'Help yourself,' he reached out and took one.

Carrie found herself watching his every move with fascination. He had the most beautiful tanned hands, with shapely, sensuous fingers, and there was something about the way he took hold of the peach and held it in the palm of his hand for a moment that made the hairs stand up on the back of her neck. Somehow, it was all too easy to imagine how it would feel to have those sensuous fingers caressing your naked flesh.

With a flash of horror at herself—what the devil was coming over her?—she pushed that thought away as he returned to their interrupted discourse and elaborated, 'I like conclusions. I hate to leave things hanging in the air.'

Carrie took a deep breath. 'Then I'll tell you why I came running after you.' Suddenly, she too was rather keen to reach a conclusion, and preferably one that involved him exiting with some rapidity. His presence was doing the most peculiar things to her brain!

Squaring her shoulders, she told him, 'I was objecting to you paying my bill. There was no need for that. I'm capable of paying my own bills.'

Leone narrowed his eyes. 'I thought that's what you were saying. But you seemed so het up I wondered if I was mistaken.'

'Of course I was het up. You had no business paying my bill for me.'

'It was a gesture of reparation. Because you lost your table.'

'Well, it was a gesture I didn't appreciate. It simply added insult to injury.' Carrie flushed in remembrance as she said it. For it really was true. She really had felt insulted. 'I came after you to complain and to insist on paying you back.'

As she spoke she sat forward, intending to stand up. 'In fact, I'll take the opportunity to pay you back now.' Over the past couple of days, the incident had continued to trouble her. How did you pay back a debt to the heir to the throne? Did you just stick some money in an envelope and send it off to the palace? How could you be certain he'd actually received it? She'd been planning on asking someone at the bank what she should do, but now the problem could be easily resolved.

She told him, 'I'll go and get the money right this minute.'

But Leone was waving to her to sit down. 'You can give it to me before I leave.' He took a bite of his peach. 'That is, if you insist, which I'd rather you didn't.'

'Well, I'm afraid I definitely do.'

Carrie was half out of her chair and half in it. It went against the grain to obey that imperious little wave, for he was clearly far too used to people obeying him, but she had suddenly realised that to go indoors for her purse she would have to step over his outstretched legs. Unless, of course, he moved them, but she couldn't bank on that.

Feeling a little cowardly, she sat back stiffly in her seat again. 'Very well,' she said. 'I'll pay you before you leave.' That surely shouldn't be long now, she was silently praying. And there was definitely no danger that she might forget.

There was silence for a moment as Leone sat back and looked at her. The more he discovered about this girl, the more intriguing she became to him. She was different, a type he came across rarely.

'You're the independent sort, I see.' His tone was light as he challenged her. 'Is this how they teach you to be over in Colorado?'

'I suppose it must be. It's certainly how I was taught.'

Carrie wondered if he was laughing at her and decided he probably was. The sort of personal integrity her parents had instilled in her ever since she was very little was something he would find petty and bourgeois and boring. People of his social rank operated differently. They were the sort of people, after all, who went through life thinking nothing of commandeering other people's restaurant tables!

She tilted her chin at him. 'I was brought up to respect people, to respect their rights, not to take advantage.' And as she looked into his eyes she could see quite clearly that he had understood the unspoken message. 'I was also taught to pay my way and to honour my debts. In short, not to take anything that wasn't my due.'

Leone regarded her with interest. 'So, what do you consider to be your due?'

'What I work for. What I earn by my own efforts.'

She paused and dropped her eyes to her lap for a moment. Was she overdoing it just a little? she wondered, suddenly guilty. She was talking, after all, to one of the idle aristocracy and she had also been taught never to give gratuitous offence.

But Leone did not appear to be offended in the slightest. Instead, he took another bite of his peach and commented, 'An extremely worthy philosophy of life.'

Not that he meant it, of course, and he could afford to smile indulgently and not care a damn what people like her thought of him. This thought went through Carrie's head as she looked into the blue eyes, observing to herself what different worlds they came from. Surely neither could ever truly understand the other?

She said, 'It's what I was taught and it's what I believe.'

Leone continued to watch her, the blue eyes oddly unsettling. They had this quality of seeming to pierce beneath her skin. At times he seemed to be laughing at her, at others studying her closely, and somehow the two just didn't add up.

What was going on in his head and why had he come? For she still wasn't convinced by the reason he'd given her. But the thing that was making her most uncomfortable of all was the fact that there seemed to be no sign of him leaving!

He crossed his feet at the ankles and tilted his head as he looked at her. 'So, what are you doing here in decadent old Europe rubbing shoulders with the sort of people I'd have thought you'd run a mile from?'

He was definitely laughing at her now. The blue eyes sparked with devilment. 'Wouldn't you have been better off choosing a different subject for your book? Something that kept you safe among the high principles of Colorado?'

Arrogant pig. Carrie looked back at him levelly. 'Actually, I don't live in Colorado any more.'

That was just for the record. He didn't know everything, after all!

'For the past three years,' she continued, 'I've lived in New York. So, you see, I have actually ventured out of the safe haven of my home state.'

'That must have been quite a jolt.' Leone was still smiling at her amusedly. 'How on earth do you manage to survive among the sharks of New York?'

'I just basically put my head down and get on with my job, just as millions of other New Yorkers do. I've never had any trouble *surviving*, as you put it.' And it was true—she'd made the shift to the Big Apple with no problem. 'Most New Yorkers, like me, believe in the ethos of hard work.'

'Back to that old subject again.' Leone lifted one dark eyebrow. 'I get the feeling that with you everything comes back to work.'

'I suppose it does, more or less. Work is a large part of my life.' And she couldn't resist adding, whether it offended him or not, 'No doubt that's a totally alien concept to you?'

'Totally.' Leone took another bite of his peach. 'I consider my life to be for living.'

Well, she knew what he meant by that! For 'living' substitute 'loving'. In the pursuit of sexual adventures was how Leone Montecrespi spent his time!

She threw him a condescending look. 'Each to his own, of course. Personally, I prefer a little more substance to my existence.'

'And who says my life lacks substance? I would say it had substance to spare.'

'Well, there's substance and substance, I suppose.' Carrie shrugged an expressive shrug. 'As I said before, each to his own.'

'Each to his own indeed.' Leone continued to watch her. And though he was smiling there was a dark, probing look in his eyes. 'Is it really true, then?' he asked, finishing off his peach and tossing the stone down on the table. 'Is work the only thing that turns you on?'

Those were not the precise words Carrie herself would have chosen, though she was not at all surprised that he had opted for that wording. It was perfectly clear that he was out to needle her.

She regarded him coolly. 'I find my work stimulating.' If he thought he could fluster her, he had another think coming. After three years in New York she didn't fluster so easily. 'Most people,' she added, 'who have jobs they're truly involved in would agree, I think, that work gives a lot of satisfaction.'

She didn't bother to add this time that he no doubt found that an alien concept. It didn't need saying. They both knew it was true. For though she'd heard he had a job—something to do with Formula One racing cars—it was clearly nothing more than a rich man's pastime. An undemanding and conveniently part-time pastime that left him plenty of free time for 'living'.

'So I've heard.' Leone was enjoying this little skirmish. 'But a lot of satisfaction is one thing; total satisfaction is quite another. And I'm beginning to suspect that you fall into the latter category.'

'Are you indeed?'

'Yes, I am. Am I right?'

Carrie fixed him with a look. Was he asking her about her sex life? Well, she was keeping that to herself—not that there was a great deal to divulge. A couple of mild romances, a few flirtations and not much more. Certainly nothing that would stand comparison with his love life!

She held the deep blue gaze. 'That's something you'll never know.'

'Top secret, huh?'

'Just my own private business.'

'Too bad. I was hoping for some intimate little insight.'

'Then I'm afraid I must disappoint you.'

'That's the worst thing you could do to me.' He smiled. 'I can't bear it when a woman disappoints me.'

Carrie could think of no reply and, really, it was little wonder, for all at once her heart was beating strangely. There was a rapid pulse in her throat and her breathing was fast and shallow. Wrong again, she was thinking. Who said she couldn't be flustered?

For there'd been an undercurrent in that exchange that had been distinctly sexual and she'd found herself responding with a sudden sense of excitement. But an excitement touched with guilt, for she'd known she shouldn't be reacting to him like that. Only she'd been unable to stop herself and had had no desire to stop him. As they sat looking at each other now, the air around them seemed to crackle.

Then Leone said, 'So you've come to San Rinaldo looking for satisfaction? Professional satisfaction, I mean, of course.' The blue eyes flashed. 'After all, we've more or less established that for you that's the only kind of satisfaction worth pursuing.'

Carrie swallowed hard. How on earth, she was wondering, had the conversation managed to arrive at this loaded point? Though she had a small suspicion that the responsibility was partly hers. For it had somehow grown out of the disapproving noises she'd made regarding his claim that life was for living.

She made a mental note to be more cautious in future. The heir to the throne clearly had no scruples at all about baiting young women who took a disapproving tone with him. Not that that knowledge would actually be of any use to her. She was unlikely ever to meet him again.

Just to think that was a great relief. She straightened her shoulders. And perhaps now she could persuade him to put an end to this meeting.

She looked across at him, though avoiding looking too deeply into his eyes. Those smouldering lapis eyes, she was learning, were dangerous. She smiled a neutral smile. 'Now that you've told me why you came here... and now that I've had a chance to explain about the other evening... it would seem your unfinished business has been completed.'

Well, that was plain enough. As hints went, that one was yacht-sized. Politely, she waited. With any luck he'd make a move now, then she could just give him his money and wave a thankful goodbye.

And he did start to stand up. At least, that was what it looked like. He sat forward in his seat, his hands on the chair arms. 'You're right; that particular piece of business has been completed.'

But then, midway, he paused, the smoky blue eyes fixing her. 'But that wasn't the only reason I came here,' he said.

Oh, dear. Carrie stiffened. Had her initial suspicions been right? Was there seduction on the royal mind, after all? She looked into his eyes and felt herself shiver. Now, how was she going to get out of this?

'Oh?' she responded, and got ready to defend herself.

Leone was watching her. 'I promise you you're going to like this.'

Carrie's insides twisted. Oh, no, I'm not, she thought.

Then he smiled. 'I know you'll like it because it happens to concern your work.'

'My work?'

'Yes, your work. I may be able to help you.'

'Help me?' She was suspicious. 'In what way?' she queried. 'I really don't think I need any help.' She hurried on, assuring him, 'I've already seen Dr Lamberti—he's the manager at the Castello factory— and we've agreed on a programme for doing interviews and photographs, plus all the access I need to the archives. I know enough Italian to decipher most of it, but if I have any problems he's offered to provide a translator.

'So, you see,' she ended, conclusively stamping on his suggestion, 'I really don't see how you could possibly help me.'

The very last thing she either needed or wanted was to get tied up with Count Leone!

He had listened without a word and now he shrugged as though in agreement. 'I guess you're right,' he told her. 'You don't need my assistance.' And, to Carrie's immense relief, he stood up.

Carrie jumped to her feet too. What joy! He was finally leaving! She couldn't wait to wave him down the stairs to his car.

But, just as he was about to head for those very same stairs, he paused and turned round to face her again. 'I take it, then,' he said with an inquisitorial lift of one eyebrow, 'that you're unaware of the existence of the Montecrespi dinner service?'

Carrie had very nearly gone walking into him when he had turned round so suddenly, and she'd been about to deliver him a fierce scowl as she stepped back. But now she forgot about scowling and blinked at him instead.

'On the contrary,' she informed him. 'I'm very much aware of the existence of the Montecrespi dinner service.'

Anyone who was even remotely interested in Castello porcelain couldn't help but know about the fabulous dinner service that had been made to mark the wedding of the first Duke back at the end of the seventeenth century.

She looked at Leone now, wondering what he was getting at. 'It's in the Duke's private collection that's kept locked up in the Palazzo Verde.' As she said it she couldn't disguise the note of longing in her voice, for she had applied to the palace press office for permission to include it in her book and had been greeted with an immediate and categorical refusal.

'But no one's allowed to see it, let alone photograph it,' she added now. For at least there had been that much consolation—that no other member of the public had ever been allowed anywhere near it either.

She kept her eyes fixed on Leone, suddenly curious. 'Why do you mention it?' she wanted to know.

'I just wondered if you'd be interested . . .'

'Interested? How do you mean, interested?'

'Interested in including it in this book of yours.'

Carrie's heart almost stopped. That look in his eyes was the look of someone holding out a bar of candy to a baby. And this was one bar of candy Carrie desperately wanted.

She swallowed and held her breath. 'But I just told you no one's allowed to see it. I already tried and they turned me down.'

'Ah, yes.' Leone smiled. 'But you didn't have me backing you then.'

Carrie was still holding her breath. 'Meaning?' she croaked.

'Meaning that if you had me backing you you might have a different response.'

'And why should you back me?'

'Do I need an ulterior motive?' His smile was pure innocence, but there was a wicked glint in his eyes. 'Maybe I'd simply like to help you,' he suggested.

Yes, and cats might kiss canaries. She didn't believe that for a second. But for now his motives were a separate issue. The issue that concerned Carrie now was much more immediate.

She let out her breath and put to him, 'Do you really mean it? Would you help me?'

'I might. And if I do there's a good chance that I'll succeed. I have a fair amount of influence with my brother.'

'If you could, that would be wonderful.' Carrie wasn't sure she should be saying this. She had the feeling that some silken noose was about to close around her neck. But how could she respond otherwise? He was offering her a prize she'd dreamed of. 'I'd really be grateful,' she heard herself add.

'Would you? That's nice to know.' Leone was still standing over her, looking down at her with eyes as tempting as Satan's. 'I'll bear that in mind,' he added, his blue gaze sweeping over her. 'A woman's gratitude, I find, is always a most generous thing. And I'm sure I'll think of a suitable way for you to express yours when the time comes.'

Carrie was about to step back. Suddenly, danger signs were flashing. And she was tempted to blurt out, Forget it! I've changed my mind! She could almost feel the silken strands of the noose biting into her neck already.

But, before she could utter a word, Leone was stepping away from her. 'I'll be in touch,' he was saying. 'Thanks for the peach.'

Then he was turning away and hurrying down the stone steps. And Carrie was still standing there, wondering what on earth she'd let herself in for, when a moment later she heard his car drive away.

*　　*　　*

Four days passed and there was no further word from him.

He's forgotten, Carrie decided, or else he was never serious in the first place. All of which was to be expected and was probably for the best anyway. Count Leone, she had decided, was as dangerous as a ticking time bomb.

So it looked as though the only reason he'd come to her house was in order to amuse himself for half an hour. How odd, she thought, when he could have been somewhere more exciting, posing for the paparazzi and making headlines for the papers. Well, perhaps he'd just felt like a quiet interlude. No doubt such were the ways of the idle aristocracy!

It was disappointing, of course, about the Montecrespi dinner service. To have been able to include that in her book would have been a major coup and she'd already been picturing it adorning the front cover! Too bad, she thought philosophically; it had been nice to dream for a while—though it had occurred to her that it might be worth having another go herself at trying to get the Duke's permission.

If I don't hear from Leone within the week I'll contact the palace press office again, she told herself. It was worth a try and she had nothing to lose.

At the same time, if she didn't hear from him she'd send off the money she owed him—for the other day, to her chagrin, it had completely slipped her mind. She'd get a money order from the bank and send it to the palace.

In the meantime she was being kept busy with her work at the Castello factory. Dr Lamberti, who had given her her own little office there, was proving to be enormously helpful and she had already taken a couple of rolls of photographs. Even without the fabulous dinner service she had the makings of a first-class book.

But the following day she was in for a small shock.

She got home from the factory to find her landlady waiting for her. 'This is for you,' Signora Rossi told her, handing her a letter. 'It was delivered this afternoon by private messenger.' She pointed to a finely embossed emblem in the corner and gave Carrie a look of bemused admiration. 'It looks as though it's come from the Palazzo Verde.'

Carrie hurried up to her bedroom and sat down on the edge of her bed before tearing the envelope open with curious fingers. Then she pulled out the single sheet of cream-coloured vellum, unfolded it carefully and began to read the message, written in a clear, plain hand.

Dear Carrie,

I've spoken to my brother on the subject we discussed. Please come to the palace on Friday evening if you wish to pursue the matter further. If not, phone the number at the top of this letter. If I don't hear from you I shall send a car to pick you up at eight-thirty.

The letter was signed quite simply, 'Leone.'

Well, how about that? She felt her heart flip over. The playboy count had kept his promise, after all, and it looked as though she was on the point of achieving her goal to include the fabulous Montecrespi dinner service in her book!

She jumped from the bed and let out a whoop of delight. I've done it! she told herself. The scoop of a lifetime!

But through her excitement there was another emotion taking hold of her. A very strong sense of apprehension. For she was remembering what Leone had said about the gratitude of women and how he would think of a suitable way for her to express hers.

Well, he's misjudged badly this time, Carrie told herself firmly. All he'll get from me is a polite and heartfelt thank-you—and maybe, if he's good, a bottle of best brandy!

But in spite of her resolution she couldn't quite conquer the way she kept feeling that familiar rush inside her every time she thought of seeing him again.

CHAPTER THREE

LEONE pushed aside the plastic curtain and stepped under the shower, feeling the cool, needle-fine jets sharp and refreshing against his back. It had been a hot, exhausting day and he had been looking forward to this.

For most of the past nine hours he'd been at the wheel of the team's racing car, doing lap after gruelling lap round the sun-scorched race circuit as he carried out rigorous tests on the new gearbox they were working on. But although it had been exhausting he felt satisfied, and as he washed the grime from his body he had a feeling of immense satisfaction at a job well done.

This was how Leone spent most of his days, down at the workshop he shared with his five team mates, either working at the drawing board or in the cockpit of one of their cars. And if he'd been able to have his way he'd have been there every day.

Some days, however, his royal duties as the Duke's brother made that ambition, sadly, impossible. There would be functions to attend or official visitors to receive and, though he tried to keep these engagements to a minimum, inevitably there were days when they intruded. But he always made a point of making up for the lost hours, coming into the workshop at dawn sometimes, at other times staying on till well after midnight. And he made the sacrifice gladly, for he adored his work.

Partly what he loved about it was the privacy and the informality. Only a very trusted few knew about his secret passion and here at the workshop he was safe from the paparazzi. And to the men with whom he worked he was an engineer, not a count. There was no time-wasting protocol. They all just got on with the job.

He turned his face to the shower and let the water splash over his head and shoulders. He had achieved a lot today—in spite, he thought, smiling, of the somewhat distracting thoughts that had kept jumping into his head, surprising him by their insistence and by the way they made him feel. Somehow, these thoughts had simply given him an extra boost.

Carrie. The elusive Carrie. She'd been in his thoughts constantly. That lovely bright-eyed face, that sexy cropped blonde hair, those glorious legs that went on for ever. There was nothing else for it. He simply had to have her.

He soaped himself quickly, strong, suntanned hands working the lather over his powerfully muscled body. For, though he was not prone to dwell on the fact, the life he had chosen to lead had equipped him with a physique that was the envy of many men—not to mention the desire of countless women. Physically, he was quite sublime, as hard-muscled as a cougar, as generously proportioned as a stallion.

Quickly, he sluiced the soap away, stepped out of the shower and reached for the towel that hung from a hook on the wall behind him. And as he rubbed himself dry Leone reflected for a moment on the note he had asked Silvestro to deliver to Carrie yesterday.

So far there'd been no phone call to say she wouldn't be coming—he'd checked with the palace during his fifteen-minute lunch break!—so it looked as though she'd be showing up tonight after all. He felt a dart inside him. It looked as though his plan was working.

He tossed the wet towel into the laundry bin where he'd already dumped his dirty overalls and crossed to the bench where his clean clothes lay. Perhaps he was being a trifle devious in the way he had chosen to lure Carrie, he reflected a little guiltily as he started to get dressed. But he had understood immediately that she was different from the others, that ordinary, more direct tactics simply wouldn't work.

Dressed now, Leone ran his fingers quickly through his hair and headed out of the locker room, glancing quickly at his watch. In just a couple of hours or so he would see her again. At the thought he felt his senses leap with pleasure.

And he quickly doused his guilty conscience. All that mattered was that he must have her. And sometimes, he decided, the end justified the means.

Carrie had taken more than an hour and a half to get dressed.

This wasn't like her at all. Normally, she was decisive in such matters. Normally, she just opened her wardrobe, pulled out something appropriate, quickly slipped it on and thought no more about it. But what did you wear for an appointment at the palace of a royal duke? None of the outfits she kept trying and retrying looked right.

And Leone's note had been vague. Would she be meeting the Duke? Would there be other people present or would it be just her and Leone? Was this to be an informal encounter or something more weighty? Would she be invited to stay for dinner?

In the end, she decided to opt for simplicity. A cool cream-coloured shift dress worn with a navy belt and navy shoes. Surely she couldn't go wrong with that?

At least Signora Rossi, her landlady, approved.

'How beautiful you look. So very chic, *signorina*.' She kissed her bunched fingertips in graphic appreciation before continuing with the real reason she'd come up to knock on Carrie's door.

'There's a car waiting downstairs for you, *signorina*.' And her eyes filled again with that amazed, admiring look that Carrie was rapidly growing used to as she added, 'It's a very big one—a limousine. I have a feeling it's from the palace.'

'Thank you, Signora Rossi.'

Carrie felt her stomach tighten. She'd been planning to be waiting out on the veranda when the car arrived, feeling cool and calm and perfectly prepared for the evening ahead. But instead, when Signora Rossi's tap had sounded on her door, she'd been rushing around, one shoe on and one shoe off, feeling anything but calm and cool.

Still, she was making a convincing effort to appear so now as she asked her landlady, 'Would you mind doing me a favour? Would you tell the driver I'll be down in just a minute?'

As Signora Rossi scuttled off, only too delighted to act as intermediary between her tenant and the palace, Carrie rushed over to the mirror for a final quick check. Not perfect, but not too bad, she thought. And it would just have to do!

She crossed her fingers. 'Here goes!' she told herself, grabbing her navy bag and heading for the door.

It was about a twenty-minute drive to the Palazzo Verde, first down the winding road that led to the city, then round the edge of the bay, sparkling silver in the moonlight, and upwards again to the spectacular promontory where the three-hundred-year-old Palazzo Verde stood.

As they approached it, Carrie held her breath. Suddenly, her previous anxiety had transformed itself into sheer excitement. Who would ever have thought she'd be setting foot in the palace, and as a guest, no less, of the ruling family itself? No doubt about it, this was going to be a night to remember!

And what made it doubly special was what was destined to come out of it, of course. The jealously guarded Montecrespi dinner service was about to be made available to her for inclusion in her book!

The limousine swept to a halt in a huge paved courtyard, green with potted plants and tall, waving palm trees, and a moment later, before she could even wonder what to do next, the driver was jumping out and coming round to open the door for her.

'Prego, signorina,' he murmured.

Carrie climbed out, trying not to beam at the wonder of it all, for the floodlit palace was really quite breathtaking this close up, its turrets and pediments and graceful arches glowing rosy gold and gloriously ancient.

'*Grazie,*' she murmured back, glancing happily round her. It felt like a privilege just to be in such a place.

A huge double wooden door was standing open, and beyond it Carrie could see the sumptuous interior of the palace. A vast circular entrance hall lit by crystal chandeliers that made the rug-strewn marble floor gleam like a mirror. This was a far cry, she was thinking, from the modest stone house she had been brought up in, or even from her smart little apartment in New York. Inwardly, she laughed. This was really living!

A woman in a dark suit seemed to appear from nowhere as she crossed the open doorway and stepped into the huge hall. She smiled welcomingly at Carrie. 'Miss Carrie Dunn?' she asked politely. Then, as Carrie nodded, she informed her, 'I'm Flavia. Please come with me.'

Her heels tapping against the marble, Carrie followed the woman across the hall and down a series of wide, bright corridors. And as she went her eyes were darting to left and to right, trying to take in just a fraction of the treasures—precious porcelain and gleaming silver, antique bronzes and old masters—that were arranged on the antique furniture or hanging on the walls. She could feel her head spinning with the wonder of it all.

Then Flavia stood aside to allow her to step through a doorway and Carrie forgot her spinning head as her heart stopped in her chest.

'You made it. It's good to see you.'

Leone was standing before her in a room all decked out in blue and silver. But it wasn't the beauty of the decor that had made her heart stop, it was the sight of Leone in his softly cut dark suit, looking ten times more magnificent than any mortal had a right to.

He stepped towards her, took her lightly by the arms and kissed each cheek. 'Take a seat. Make yourself comfortable. Let me offer you a drink.'

Carrie was grateful for the invitation. She was having difficulty standing, even though her poor heart had started beating again. Tearing her eyes from him and fighting to regain her composure, she sank down thankfully into the nearest armchair.

What a fool you are, she was thinking crossly to herself. OK, he's gorgeous, but for heaven's sake pull yourself together. Try to remember he's only gorgeous on the outside!

'What will you have?'

He was standing over her. Her heart flickered again, dangerously, as she caught the cool, clean scent of him.

She forced herself to glance up, steeling herself as she did so. 'Just mineral water, please.' And she sighed inwardly with relief. She was back in control again. Her heart was beating normally.

'Just mineral water? You wouldn't rather have something a little stronger?' He was crossing to a table where an array of bottles and glasses were laid out, his movements, she observed, as smooth and lithe as a cat's.

She pushed that thought away. 'No, just mineral water, thank you. I'm not a great consumer of alcohol.'

'Neither am I.' He smiled at her. 'I like to keep a clear head. But it's been a hard day. I think I deserve a glass of champagne.'

'A hard day'. Carrie made no comment but she grimaced inwardly. It wasn't too difficult to imagine what his 'hard day' had consisted of. A couple of meetings in the morning with various palace flunkies in order to dish out his orders for the day, then a nice long lunch at some private club or other and the afternoon spent lazing around with friends.

She regarded him sceptically. To tell the truth, she was surprised to see him pouring their drinks himself. She'd assumed he'd leave such menial tasks to the servants.

But then there were no servants around. Not a single one. A thought struck her. Maybe he didn't want servants around right now. Perhaps he had sent them away because he wanted to be alone with her. Flavia, after all, had disappeared pretty sharpish, discreetly closing the door as she went.

As Leone turned suddenly to glance at her, Carrie felt a dart in her chest, remembering again what he'd told her that day about how she might express her gratitude. Was that what this private little drink was leading up to? For it looked as though there was going to be just the two of them, after all.

He was coming towards her, holding out a crystal glass. 'Your mineral water,' he said, reaching out to hand it to her, his fingers brushing lightly against hers as he did so.

'Thank you.'

Carrie resisted the urge to snatch her hand away. She had no desire to spill her drink and make a fool of herself. Besides, she had nothing to worry about. He hadn't delivered the goods yet, and even when he did all he would get for his pains would be a sincere verbal thank-you and a bottle of brandy. If he had seduction on his mind, he was about to be sorely disappointed.

Rather relishing this prospect, she took a sip of her drink and glanced admiringly round the room.

'This is a beautiful room. In fact, the whole palace is beautiful. At least, the bits I've seen this evening.'

A bit of polite conversation was probably called for, she decided, before they got down to discussing business. Besides, it was true. The palace was quite stunning.

Leone followed her gaze. 'Yes, it is rather beautiful. The whole place was redecorated just over two years ago. It was a major project of my mother's. She completed it just before she died.'

There was a note in his voice that made Carrie turn and look at him. It had been carefully controlled, but it had definitely been there. A note of sadness, a note of grief. It had caught her unawares.

Carrie knew that his mother had died very suddenly just over a year after the death of his father, the old Duke. That was a terrible double tragedy for any son to bear but, perhaps foolishly, she had assumed that the playboy count would be unaffected. And that was clearly not the case. So he was human after all.

But the moment was soon gone. Even as she turned to look at him he was seating himself in one of the armchairs opposite her and smiling as he took a mouthful of his champagne. 'So,' he was saying, 'do you reckon she did a good job?'

Carrie ignored the smile in his voice. He was probably laughing at her again, finding it amusing that she should set herself up as a judge of such things. But she didn't care. She was entitled to her opinion.

'I think she did a wonderful job,' she answered. 'Like I said, the palace is beautiful.'

'I could arrange to show you round some time, let you see the rest of it. That is, if you're interested in seeing old houses.'

Old houses! Carrie laughed inwardly. Well, that was one way of describing it—though she could see that it probably was just a house to him. The house he had been brought up in. The house he lived in even now.

'I'd love that,' she said. And as she said it she eyed him. I wonder how he'll expect me to express my gratitude for *that* favour?

And it was then that she remembered she had something to give him.

She reached for her bag. 'I've brought that money I owe you. The other day you went away without it.'

Leone smiled. 'Yes, so I did, and I'd forgotten all about it. But you evidently hadn't. How extraordinarily fastidious of you.'

Before she could stop herself Carrie smiled back at him. That was the phrase she'd once used of him. Still smiling, she paraphrased the reply he had given her.

'I happen to be an extremely fastidious girl.'

But instantly she wished she hadn't said it. Even to her own ears it had sounded decidedly flirtatious, and surely that was the last thing she was trying to be?

And she felt her insides curl as one dark eyebrow lifted. 'So we have something in common? Well, that's a start, I'd say.'

Then he just sat there watching her, the dark blue eyes unblinking, seeming to draw her like a magnet across the room. Carrie felt a sudden panic and dropped her own gaze quickly. She would drown in those seductive blue eyes if she wasn't careful.

She fumbled with her bag and hurriedly changed the subject. 'Let me give you that money now.' And she began to scrabble for her wallet.

Though even as she scrabbled she was doubting the wisdom of this move. What she wanted was to widen the gap between them, not narrow it! And here she was proposing to get out of her chair, walk across the room and press a wad of money into his hand!

She had a sudden vision of what might happen if she did. She saw him reach out and catch hold of her and pull her into his arms. She felt his arms swoop tightly round her. She felt his lips crushing hers.

At this vision she held her breath, aware that her heart was pumping. She couldn't possibly risk that. She'd have to be crazy. So, she just sat there, paralysed, squirming inwardly, feeling the blue eyes on her, sensing he was waiting, every muscle in her body aching with tension.

And then, at that very moment, the door of the room burst open.

'Sorry I'm late. I got caught up in traffic. Boy, I need a drink. Be an angel, Leone.'

A young woman with light brown hair that fell in a sharp bob to her shoulders was suddenly standing, bright-eyed and breathless, between them. And as

Carrie blinked at her, delighted at this timely interruption, she recognised instantly who her saviour was.

It was Lady Caterina, Leone's sister, the youngest of the three Montecrespi siblings, and she was far more lovely than her photographs. Blue-eyed and willowy, her skin creamy and flawless, she exuded the same restless energy as her brother, but there was a totally feminine warmth about her as well. As she looked into her face, Carrie liked her instantly.

Caterina was coming over to introduce herself. 'Sorry I'm late,' she was saying. 'I was supposed to be here to greet you, but you know how it is... I've just been running late all day.'

Carrie rose to shake her hand and smiled in response. 'I know exactly what you mean. I often have days like that myself.'

And the remark was sincere, for she knew from what she'd read that Caterina, unlike her playboy brother, was a hard-working young woman, involved in a whole string of charities, to which she dedicated a huge chunk of her time. She couldn't be more different from Leone. They were chalk and cheese.

Caterina was seating herself in a nearby armchair. 'I hear you're an American,' she was saying. 'I love America. It's one of my favourite countries. And I adore the people. They're so open and generous.'

Two things were suddenly striking Carrie as she turned with a smile to accept all this praise on behalf of her fellow countrymen. One was what Caterina had said just a moment ago—that she'd been supposed to be here at the palace to greet her—which meant, after all, that it had not been Leone's plan to get Carrie on her own in order to seduce her. That, it would seem, had all been in her head!

And the other thing that was striking her was the way Leone had responded to his sister's request to be an angel and fix her a drink. The angel bit was possibly pushing it, but he hadn't hesitated to oblige. And now he was coming across to deliver her drink to her, totally naturally, as though he did it all the time. And maybe he did, Carrie conceded grudgingly. Maybe he wasn't a total waster, after all.

'Here you are. One extremely dry Martini.' He handed it over, then he turned to address Carrie. 'Would you like me to top up your mineral water?'

Carrie had been carefully avoiding looking him in the face, for something else had struck her, something she found deeply worrying. But she had to look at him now, though she kept the eye contact brief. 'No, thanks. I'm fine,' she said, answering his question.

But, in spite of her care to glance away quickly, one look in his eyes had started her heart clattering—for she'd been thinking of that scandalous fantasy of a few moments ago. The fantasy in which, when she'd crossed to hand him the money, he'd grabbed her, hauled her into his arms and devastated her with a kiss. Since he'd been expecting his sister to arrive at any moment, it was unlikely that anything could have been further from his mind. The only mind that shameless fantasy had been in was her own!

Carrie felt herself squirm. Where were these disgraceful thoughts coming from? She must pull herself together and stop reacting to him like this.

Caterina was saying now, addressing her brother, 'Is Damiano dropping in? Is he back from that meeting yet?'

'He said he'd drop by.' Leone reseated himself in his armchair. 'But I don't know if he's back yet. These meetings can go on a bit.'

'You mean he's coming here?'

Carrie glanced up expectantly. It looked as though she was going to meet the Duke, after all. My word! she was thinking. This is quite a scoop. First a count then a lady and now a royal duke!

'I thought it would be an idea for you to meet him.'

As he said it, Leone glanced across at her and winked. And there was something about that wink, something so decidedly conspiratorial that Carrie swallowed back the questions that had been rising to her lips.

Has he actually given the OK? Is he coming just to discuss the details? Or is he still making up his mind about it?

But she kept these queries to herself, at least for the moment. For she sensed that with that wink Leone had been warning her to keep their business between themselves and not discuss it in front of Caterina. That struck her as a little odd, but presumably he had his reasons.

And it was quite clear that Caterina knew nothing of their business as she turned now to face Carrie and proceeded to explain, 'The three of us often meet down here for an evening drink. We all have our separate apartments, of course, but we try to keep in touch.' Then she glanced across at Leone. 'Do you think Sofia will be joining us? It's ages since she showed her face.'

Leone shrugged. 'Maybe she's not feeling so good. She is pregnant, after all.'

Carrie felt her ears prick up with interest. The Sofia they were speaking about was the Duke's beautiful young wife, who was currently pregnant with the couple's first baby. It had been in all the newspapers just a couple of months ago.

'I don't think it's got anything to do with her being pregnant. If you ask me,' Caterina chipped in again, 'there's something wrong with that girl. I worry about her. She just doesn't look happy.'

Carrie tried to look as though she wasn't listening. These people were public figures whose lives were regularly splashed across the newspapers, but this was private family stuff they were discussing and she felt a little uncomfortable about listening in.

Brother and sister evidently thought the same—that it was an inappropriate subject for discussion—for it was instantly dropped and they moved on to other things, with Caterina advising Carrie on all the things she should go and see during her stay in San Rinaldo. And it was all thoroughly entertaining. Carrie enjoyed herself immensely.

And it seemed that Caterina had too. 'I hope we meet again,' she told Carrie as she finally took her leave of them about half an hour later.

Even with Caterina gone, Carrie continued to feel quite relaxed. Her previous tension had completely vanished. And to her astonishment she had actually found Leone good company—humorous and amusing and not arrogant at all. The role of good-natured older brother definitely rather suited him. Why, she had almost stopped thinking of him as a rampant seducer!

'Let me make a quick phone call.' He rose to his feet now and crossed to the phone on a small table in the far corner. 'I want to find out what's happened to Damiano.'

Carrie watched him as he conducted a brief conversation in Italian, wishing she had a better mastery of the spoken language. With the aid of a large dictionary she could decipher the written language, but her ears hadn't quite adapted to speech yet. She could pick out a few words here and there, but not enough to know what he was really saying.

Still, it was a pleasure just to listen. It was a beautiful language anyway, but, quite frankly, the way Leone spoke it sent shivers down her back.

Oh, dear! She bit her lip at that. She was supposed to have stopped that sort of thinking! It was far too dangerous. She was supposed to be taking control of herself!

Leone had finished his conversation and was coming towards her. 'I think we ought to go and eat now,' he was saying. 'I don't know about you, but I'm feeling pretty hungry.'

Carrie had been wondering about food, for she was feeling peckish too. But there were a couple of questions she needed answers to first before she could consider accepting his invitation. Without moving from her seat, she proceeded to ask them.

'So, what's happening about your brother? Did you manage to get in touch with him?' And, finally, the most vital question of all. 'Where exactly were you proposing that we eat?'

She had no desire to be whisked off somewhere without knowing where she was going!

Leone smiled at her caution and answered her first two questions first.

'I spoke to my brother's secretary and apparently he's still in this meeting. So I've left a message asking if he'll see us as soon as he gets back.'

Then he smiled, his eyes dancing. 'As to where I propose that we eat...' He reached out before she could stop him and drew her from her chair. 'You and I are going to have dinner in my private apartments.'

As she blinked, he took her arm and slipped it through his. 'Just the two of us, all alone. Isn't that going to be nice?'

In the event, they weren't alone. At least, not all of the time. Silvestro was there, discreetly waiting at table.

Carrie was glad of the man's presence, for her earlier feeling of ease had totally evaporated in the meantime. Dining alone with Leone, she suspected, wasn't going to be nice at all!

Needless to say, at the first opportunity she had reclaimed her arm—but not before the most excruciating attack of hot and cold tingles had gone rushing through her at that unexpected physical contact.

'If you don't mind,' she'd told him curtly, 'I can walk without your help.'

Then she'd stood awkwardly with him in the lift—Leone's apartments were on the fourth floor—her eyes on the door, studiously ignoring his amused smile, then hurtled out of it in relief when the doors had finally opened. Then she had walked behind him as he led the way to his apartments, reflecting that the oriental habit of the woman walking six paces behind her man was actually a pretty sensible one, after all. It allowed the woman to keep a sharp eye on every move the man made.

She had continued to keep a sharp eye on him as they stepped into his drawing room, a beautiful room decorated in amber and dark green, then through a wide pillared archway into a small dining room where a table stood waiting by the open balcony windows. It was spread with a fine linen cloth, with a bowl of roses in the centre, and laid for two with sparkling crystal and gleaming silver.

That was where they were seated now as Silvestro served them coffee at the end of what had been a perfectly delicious dinner.

Carrie touched her lips with her napkin. The meal had been perfect. But there was still one thing missing. There was no sign of the Duke.

She glanced across at Leone, who had been the perfect host all evening—anticipating her every wish, passing dishes and pouring wine for her, and always keeping the conversation light and easy, inviting her to tell him about her life and work in New York. Though that hadn't changed a thing. Her tension had never left her. She had gone through the motions of being as cool and relaxed as he was, but really, inside, she was as tight as a drum.

She couldn't help it. There was just something about the intimacy of the situation—in spite of Silvestro's constant coming and going—that tied her poor nervous innards up in knots.

Perhaps she was just too aware that Leone's bedroom was right next door—not that he had told her that it was; she had simply guessed. Which really summed the whole thing up. It was absolutely hopeless. She kept trying, but she was just incapable of controlling her thoughts. Put Leone within a hundred feet of her and she became obsessed with bed and sex!

At the moment, however, there was something else on her mind, something that was starting to trouble her a little.

She glanced across at Leone and said, not for the first time, though she was determined to get a straight answer out of him this time, 'Do you think your brother's coming? It's getting a bit late. Shouldn't you maybe ring his secretary again and check?'

Last time she'd said something similar he'd simply told her not to worry. And, likewise, when she had asked what the purpose of the meeting was—had he fixed things with Duke Damiano or were there still things to discuss?—he had airily assured her that it was all under control. But now she was beginning to doubt that. She had the feeling she was being fobbed off. And the feeling was making her even more tense than ever.

She watched him now as he glanced at his watch and she was aware that she was holding her coffee-cup very tight. 'Don't you think you should maybe check,' she insisted, 'that he actually got your message?'

If Leone was aware of her growing tension he did not show it.

He shrugged. 'You're right. It is getting late. I don't really think there's any point in phoning now. I reckon we'll just have to postpone the meeting.'

'Postpone it?' Carrie glared at him as anger went rushing through her. Did this mean she had endured this evening for nothing? She felt like reaching across the table and strangling him with her bare hands.

And that wasn't all. Suddenly, she was starting to feel certain that a suspicion that had been growing in her head all evening wasn't, after all, just paranoia. No meeting with his brother had ever been arranged. He had been stringing her along from start to finish.

It all added up. That was why Caterina knew nothing. And it was why he'd avoided discussing the subject. He had set her up. That phone call had been phoney. The more these thoughts seethed within her, the more certain she became.

And now he was casually saying that the meeting would have to be postponed. What a cop-out. Did he really expect her just to take this kind of treatment?

'Postpone it?' she said again, laying down her coffee-cup with a clatter. Then she demanded, 'Are you sure you've actually spoken to your brother?'

To her intense annoyance, his response was to smile. 'What's the matter? Don't you trust me?' he enquired.

'Trust you?' She was really mad now, her tension smouldering to fury. 'No, I don't, as a matter of fact. I don't trust you at all. You haven't spoken to your brother. You're just playing some game with me!'

For that would explain something else. It would explain her own strange obsession, why she kept thinking of his bedroom and feeling ill at ease with him. It was because her personal radar, some instinctive sixth sense in her, had seen through him and picked up his secret intentions. All these things were only in her mind because they'd been in his mind first. He hadn't brought her here to talk about the dinner service at all. That had simply been a lure. He had brought her here to seduce her!

Carrie threw down her napkin as she felt her anger spill over. 'You knew your brother would be busy tonight and that there'd be no chance of me meeting him! There was never any meeting arranged at all!'

As her voice rose she was rather glad that Silvestro had withdrawn and, presumably, was out of earshot. She could really go to town and tell Leone what she thought of him.

'This whole thing has been a trick! You never meant to help me! You're nothing but a lying, cheating snake!'

Leone had barely batted an eyelid. He regarded her calmly across the table. 'Why on earth,' he demanded, 'are you getting so upset?'

That was the final straw! Carrie rose furiously to her feet, fully intending to go marching out through the door. But at that very moment Silvestro appeared through it instead, stopping in his tracks at the sight of her flushed face.

Being the well-trained servant that he was, he exited immediately, but Carrie had already flung away in frustration. She couldn't sit down again now and she couldn't bear to look at Leone. So she took the only other option and flounced out onto the balcony.

The blood was roaring in her ears as she leaned against the parapet, and she could hardly see straight for the anger that seethed in her. I should never have trusted him! I should have known he'd make a fool of me! I knew what type of man he was!

There was a sudden movement behind her. She knew it was Leone. She could smell the familiar cool, clean scent of him.

Without turning to look at him, she told him, her tone a warning, 'Don't come near me or I promise you I'll throw you off this balcony.'

She felt him smile, then he spoke softly, 'What's up, Carrie? What's got into you?' A moment later he had reached out and laid a hand on her arm.

Carrie's entire body had gone rigid. She spun round. 'I warned you!' Her fists were clenched, ready to pummel him to the ground.

But something happened to her the moment she looked into his eyes. She felt her body go slack and, as his arm slipped round her waist, she simply tilted back her head and waited for him to kiss her.

CHAPTER FOUR

IT WAS a kiss that, quite simply, took her breath away.

As soft as thistledown, as warm as sunshine, as sweet as honey, as thrilling as freefall.

And freefall was a pretty good description of what it felt like. Like leaping into some void, the wind whistling past her ears, the giddy feeling that the ground was rushing up to meet her.

But then it was as though her parachute had suddenly opened. All at once she was floating. Her body had become weightless. As insubstantial and as buoyant as a cloud. It was the most magical feeling in the whole world.

As Leone's lips pressed down on hers, his arms tight around her, Carrie could feel a heat and a heaviness inside her that seemed to curl all the way from the top of her scalp right down to the coral-painted tips of her toes. The sensation held her there, immobilising her totally, and she made no effort whatsoever to fight it. What sense would there be in that? It was totally delicious.

For not only Carrie's body had become Leone's weak and willing prisoner. Her will, too, had surrendered to him with no more protest than a sigh.

Which was why her hands had floated up to rest on his shoulders, her fingers curling softly round the back of his neck. Somehow, it had just happened.

She'd had no choice in the matter. And she loved the warm feel of his flesh against her fingertips.

Her fingers were reaching up to lace through his hair now, so wonderfully cool and soft and springy. And she felt drunk with the warm scent of him. It was making her dizzy. She had never felt anything remotely like this before.

That was when a bell, belatedly, rang in her head. She should not be feeling it now. This was Leone, seducing her. And she was just standing here meekly, without a protest, letting him. Though it was much worse than that. She was actively encouraging him! A shaft of horror tore through her. Had she gone mad?

She snatched her hands from his shoulders and pressed them against her chest. 'Stop it!' she commanded, struggling to free herself. 'Stop it this instant! What the devil do you think you're doing?'

Not much struggle was required. Leone stepped back almost instantly, dropping his arms away from her waist. And as a smile touched his lips Carrie thought for a moment that he was about to make some amused, mocking comment at her expense. And she could hardly have blamed him. Her sudden outrage was a little suspect. He hadn't been the only one doing the kissing!

But he made no such comment. Instead, he said to her, 'Why were you so upset a moment ago?'

Carrie blinked at him. Upset? She couldn't recall being upset. In fact, she could recall nothing before that dynamite kiss. The powerful impact of it had washed her brain clean.

'Was I?' She frowned at him, struggling to remember.

'Extremely.'

He slipped his hands into his trouser pockets and looked down at her with humorous blue eyes. He's behaving as though nothing happened a moment ago, Carrie was thinking. And she wasn't at all sure how she felt about that.

'You threw down your napkin and came stomping out here. I seem to remember you even threatened to throw me off the balcony.'

Belatedly, a cog in Carrie's brain clicked into place. Yes, now she remembered! And as the memory flowed back she felt her anger flow back with it.

'I had every right to be upset,' she accused. 'You've been leading me up the garden path!'

'Have I?' Dark eyebrows rose. 'Kindly explain what you mean.'

He knew very well what she meant. He was just playing more games with her. Carrie took a step away from the stone balustrade of the balcony, carefully putting more distance between them. 'OK,' she conceded, 'since you insist on playing the innocent, it'll be my pleasure to explain.'

Then, as he continued to watch her, she folded her arms across her chest and proceeded to explain what he already knew. 'You promised to speak to your brother about the Montecrespi dinner service and persuade him to let me include it in my book. But you haven't, have you? It was all just a trick.'

'A trick?'

'Yes, a trick. You're playing some game with me.'

She was choosing her words carefully, reluctant to accuse him outright of using his promise as a lure to try and seduce her. If they got back onto that subject it could lead to all sorts of tricky diversions. Much wiser just to stick to what was really bothering her.

'Admit I'm right,' she insisted. 'You haven't spoken to your brother. You haven't, have you? It was all just a trick.'

But Leone was shaking his head. 'I'm afraid you're quite wrong, you know. I spoke to my brother, just as I said I would.' He frowned at her. 'What makes you think I haven't?'

Carrie squinted at him. Was this more lies? 'Are you serious?' she demanded.

'Of course I'm serious.' Leone smiled. 'I spoke to him the other night.'

Carrie was starting to feel a little foolish. Could she be wrong, after all? Her mind ranged back over what had made her suspect him in the first place. There'd been no concrete proof, really. She'd simply felt it in her bones.

She continued to regard him semi-suspiciously. 'And what did your brother say when you spoke to him?' she demanded.

'He said he'd like to meet you before he makes a definite decision—though I'm pretty sure I've convinced him to say yes. And that's why I invited you here this evening—so you could meet him and come to some arrangement. But unfortunately he's been tied up and that didn't happen.' He regarded her with unblinking blue eyes for a moment. 'You see, you really have no cause to be so distrustful.'

Didn't she? Carrie was still not totally convinced. Leone Montecrespi was as tricky as a bag of monkeys. Still, there was no point in insisting. If he was telling the truth, that would only annoy him; and if he wasn't, it wouldn't make a spit of difference anyway.

So she shrugged. 'OK, let's assume I was wrong. So, what happens now? Will you speak to him again?'

'I'll speak to him tomorrow.'

'OK. Thank you.' Then she gritted her teeth. 'I'm sorry if I was wrong about you.' It would have been a little ungracious not to apologise!

'Don't mention it.' He looked into her eyes with a smile. 'In the end, your little tantrum didn't do any harm.' As he said it he reached out and tucked a loose strand of hair behind her ear. 'On the contrary, I'd say, it proved to be quite positive.'

Well, Carrie knew what that meant! It was her 'tantrum', after all, that had led to that disgraceful, mind-blowing kiss! As his finger brushed her ear she stepped hastily away, just in case he was planning any more positive moves! And the way her ear was suddenly burning and her heart rushing inside her, she was really only half listening as he went on to add, 'In the meantime, while we're waiting for Damiano to give the go-ahead, I can arrange for you to have a look—just a look—at the dinner service.'

'That won't be necessary, thank you.'

Carrie spoke without thinking, wondering if it was his offer or his advance she was rejecting. Whichever it was, she felt a deep, fierce need to say no. For the burning in her ear had spread to her entire scalp now. He had only touched her ear lightly, but it had sparked off an explosion of sensation.

She pursed her lips at him angrily, though it was herself she was really mad at. 'Just let me know when the meeting with your brother's been set up. There's no point in me wasting time coming to see the collection before then.'

'As you wish. But if you change your mind all you have to do is ring me. The number's on that note I sent you yesterday.' He paused and held her eye. 'That is, if you still have it?'

'I may still have it somewhere.' Carrie fought back a blush as she said it. She knew precisely where it was—in the top drawer of her dressing table! She was keeping it as a memento to take home and show her parents!

'But I won't need it,' she added, dropping her eyes from his. 'As I said, I'll wait until you've fixed things with your brother.'

'Suit yourself. The offer's there.' Leone glanced at his watch. 'And now I think it's time I took you home.' He flicked her a look. 'Unless you'd like a brandy first?'

'No, thanks; I'd rather go home.' Carrie glanced at her own watch, and was astonished to see that it was already after midnight. 'I've got a busy day tomorrow,' she told him.

'Me too.' He smiled at her. 'Come on, let's go, then.'

He led her out into the corridor and down in the lift, then across the marble entrance hall and out into the courtyard. A sleek black sports car, its top down, was parked there. As Leone pulled open the passenger door, Carrie slid inside. And then, with a low growl, they were setting off through the palace gates.

Carrie was extremely glad that the top of the car was down. It was rather pleasant driving along with the wind in her hair and the scents of the clean night air in her nostrils. But, more to the point, it would have been extremely worrying to have been cooped up with Leone in such a small space. She would have had a great deal of difficulty coping with that!

As it was, she was taking pains to look nowhere near him, glad he wasn't insisting on anything but the minimum of conversation and slightly troubled by thoughts of what would happen when they got to the villa—though she had already decided how she would make certain that nothing did!

As soon as they arrived she would be out of the car like a rocket, just in case he had any notions about kissing her goodnight. There had already been more than enough kissing for one night!

They were climbing up the winding road that led to the villa and Carrie's hand was already hovering over the doorhandle. I'll just leap straight out, then say, Thank you and goodnight, she told herself firmly as the villa came into sight. And she held her breath as the car turned into the driveway, then drew to a halt as he pulled on the handbrake.

Her hand was clasping the doorhandle, but something very strange happened. She didn't push the door open and she didn't leap out. Instead, with pounding heart, she turned to face him.

'Thank you for dinner,' she told him. 'It really was lovely.' And then she just sat there, not moving a muscle.

Leone had turned to look at her. 'My pleasure,' he assured her. 'I hope we can do it again some time soon.' Then, unhurriedly, he leaned towards her and kissed her lightly on the lips.

'Goodnight,' he murmured, 'and *sogni d'oro*. Golden dreams.'

'Goodnight.'

In a kind of trance, Carrie pushed the door open. That had not been meant to happen, but she was rather pleased that it had. She stepped out on giddy legs. What a dreamy goodnight kiss!

Leone watched from the car as she climbed the steps to her front door, then he waited till the light was on and she was safely indoors. Then, returning her final wave, he swung the car out onto the road and headed back to the Palazzo Verde, his spirits soaring.

Soon she would be his. He trod hard on the gas and punched the steering wheel with the heel of his hand. His plan was working an absolute treat!

Over the next couple of days Carrie found it increasingly difficult to keep her mind on Castello porcelain.

She was spending long hours with the ever helpful Dr Lamberti and some particularly interesting members of his staff—for some of the hand-decorators at the factory belonged to families who had been working for Castello for generations.

One, old Bruno Nardi, proudly told her how he had learned his skills directly from his father who in turn had learned from his own father before him. And each Nardi son had sat at the same workbench where he sat now, decorating the fragile cups and dishes and vases with the designs that had been passed down through the centuries. Though, alas, he lamented, the

tradition would end with him. His own son had chosen
to go into banking.

On one level, Carrie was totally absorbed by it all
and absolutely delighted at the way things were going.
These personal little touches would make all the difference to her book. They would bring it alive. They
would make it special. She found her enthusiasm in-
creasing daily.

But on another level, simultaneously, she felt detached from it all. For she was finding it increasingly
impossible to block out thoughts of Leone.

He kept jumping into her consciousness at the most
unexpected moments. There she would be, bent over
some masterpiece in the little Castello museum at the
factory, and suddenly she would realise that her
thoughts were elsewhere. She wasn't thinking about
the marvellous translucency of the porcelain or of the
wonderful quality of the decoration. She was thinking
about something much more mundane and prosaic.
She was thinking about how wonderful it had been
to kiss Leone.

Though perhaps mundane and prosaic were not the
best words to describe that. Kissing Leone had been
a thrilling, lyrical experience, like nothing she had ever
experienced before.

Never before in her life had she been so swept away.
Never before had she felt her heart fly like a bird. No
wonder the experience had turned her inside out.

It was strange. Here she was, already twenty-four
years old, and this was truly the first time a man had
affected her this way. She'd felt mild attractions
before. It wouldn't have been natural if she hadn't.

She'd had boyfriends whose kisses had been perfectly pleasant. But pleasant was really as far as it had gone.

But Leone's kisses weren't pleasant. They blew her out of her shoes!

She sighed now. No doubt her innocence was to blame. When it came to men and love she really didn't have much experience. Leone had accused her once of only wanting satisfaction from her work, but that wasn't true. It wasn't true at all. Maybe she had, to some extent, put her love life on hold over the past few years while she carved out her career. But, when she met the right man, she intended to put that right.

Carrie smiled a wry smile. And Leone definitely wasn't the right man.

There was no denying that he had a staggering effect on her. But any attraction between them was destined to come to nothing. He was a count and a playboy, skilled at flirting and seduction, and she was a serious career girl with very strong ideas about love.

In her book it wasn't a game—she had been taught that and she believed it. One didn't fall into a love affair just for a bit of fun and excitement. Love and sex, she firmly believed, should be buttressed by commitment. There was no sense otherwise. It was dishonest and far too risky.

So her brief experience with Leone was destined to remain just that. It was a pity in a way, but the alternatives simply were not acceptable.

Once she had sorted that out in her mind, Carrie felt much better—in spite of the shameful thoughts that still kept intruding in her head. But they would pass soon enough. She was just going through a phase.

There had been no word from Leone since that dinner at the Palazzo Verde. On a personal level that didn't surprise her. He had masses of girlfriends. Far too many to bother seriously about acquiring one more! But on a professional level it made her anxious.

Had he spoken to his brother again, as he had promised? Her doubts were starting to crowd in again. Maybe she ought to ring him. Exert a little pressure. But she hesitated. He might think she was really ringing for something else!

Well, he was wrong. She steeled herself. If he were anyone else, she would do it. For there was no personal motive. It was strictly business. And it would be madness not to get this thing sorted out just because she'd once allowed Leone to kiss her!

Carrie phoned the same day. 'I'd like to speak to Count Leone, please,' she told the male voice that answered after a couple of rings, announcing in Italian, 'Count Leone's private office.'

'Just a minute,' Pierre told her now, switching at once to English and having a private little smile to himself—this was the American girl he'd tracked down for his boss! 'I'll see if Count Leone is available.'

He was.

'You just caught me. I was on my way out,' Leone told her when he came to the phone a couple of minutes later. Then he went on before she could say a word, 'I see you've changed your mind about coming to have a look at the dinner service. So, why not come this afternoon? Around four o'clock, say. I can arrange to show it to you then.'

Carrie was smiling. He really did sound as though he was in a rush! And though he'd got it wrong, of course—that was not why she'd called—she decided just to go along with him and go and see the dinner service anyway, for the truth was that she'd regretted her hasty refusal of that offer. And she could bring up her real reason for calling him when she saw him. He was clearly in too much of a hurry to go into all that now.

So she simply said, 'OK. Four o'clock's fine.'

When she hung up the phone she was trying very hard not to feel too excited at the prospect of seeing him. As she had told herself earlier, it was strictly business—and an opportunity, of course, to finally pay back the money she had forgotten, yet again, to hand over to him last time!

It was just folly on her part, and totally inappropriate, that her heart was suddenly beating fit to burst out of her chest, and that a grin that would surely have put the Cheshire cat to shame was currently spread across her face.

Carrie arrived at the palace at five minutes to four, seated in the back of a yellow taxi cab that was waved through the gates with no trouble at all when she gave the guards her name as Leone had instructed.

She was dressed in a blue cotton blouse and a blue and white striped skirt, and though she was no longer grinning quite so broadly as she had been earlier there was still a light in her eyes and a happy curve to her mouth. What was wrong with combining business with a bit of personal pleasure?

Flavia was waiting for her at the door with the same welcoming smile as before.

'Good afternoon, Miss Dunn. Please follow me.'

Carrie tripped along behind her, feeling perfectly at ease. She was an old hand now. She could have found her way herself. But at the end of one of the corridors Flavia turned left instead of right.

'I thought we were going to—' Carrie started to blurt out, intending to finish the sentence with 'to Count Leone's quarters'.

But Flavia was already turning round. 'I'm sorry, I should have told you. We're going to Lady Caterina's office. She's waiting for you there.'

Lady Caterina's office? Carrie felt her heart plummet inside her. Still, never mind, she told herself. Maybe Leone was there.

But Leone wasn't there. Only Caterina was waiting for her.

'Leone's asked me to stand in for him,' Caterina explained. 'He got held up. He asked me to apologise.'

Did he, indeed? Well, she didn't need his apologies. It was ridiculous how angry and disappointed Carrie felt. Like a pricked balloon. She was all churned up inside. I'm crazy, she told herself, and tried to pull herself together.

She smiled at Caterina. 'Well, thanks for standing in.'

Caterina, as it turned out, was a most knowledgeable guide. As they walked round the display cases where the dinner service was housed, she told Carrie, 'As you probably know, it was made in 1670 for the wedding of the first Duke, Cosimo, and Lady Isabella. No one knows how much it's worth. It's beyond calculation.'

That did not surprise Carrie, for it was truly magnificent. More than two thousand pieces—dinner plates, soup bowls, dessert dishes, gravy boats. It just went on and on, each piece as delicately lustrous, its gold leaf as immaculate, its painted colours as fresh and bright as they had been when it had first graced the first Duke's table.

Carrie was going weak at the knees. It was making her head spin. I've just *got* to get permission to include this in my book, she was thinking.

It seemed that Caterina had read her mind. 'Leone's been telling me,' she said suddenly, 'that you're hoping to use this in the book you're writing.' She smiled. 'I'm sure you'll get permission. Leone's very good at getting round Damiano.'

'I hope so.'

Carrie's heart flickered. So, she really had been wrong to doubt him. And the pleasure she felt wasn't confined solely to the prospect of including the fabulous dinner service in her book. It was also pleasure just to know that Leone hadn't been playing with her. And it was a little unsettling just how pleased that made her feel.

At last, Caterina was leading her back to her office.

In the doorway she paused. 'How about a cup of tea now?' She smiled a friendly smile. 'A cup of tea and a chat. I'm dying to get to know you better.'

Carrie was delighted to agree. 'Sure,' she said. 'I'd love to.'

So the two girls ended up spending a good hour and a half together over two pots of Earl Grey and the best part of a tin of biscuits.

And their little chat turned out to be most illuminating. For by the time—just before seven—that Carrie climbed into her taxi and made her way across the city towards home she'd been regaled with a whole mass of information—about Caterina and her work and her love life and all sorts of things, though the most fascinating topic they'd touched on had been Leone.

And what Carrie had learned about him had left her feeling quite shocked and wondering if she wouldn't have preferred to have been left in blissful ignorance.

She frowned to herself as the taxi sped up the hill, winding its way beneath the trees towards the villa. She would feel most peculiar now having to look Leone in the face. Though perhaps, she comforted herself, that wouldn't be necessary. Now that she had established a kind of friendship with Caterina, perhaps all communications could be made through his sister. Yes, that was the solution. She nodded to herself sagely. For it would be better if she never saw Leone again.

She focused on that thought. It was a wise judgement, she decided. She must steer clear of him. It was the only way she would be safe.

The villa was coming into view. She sat forward in her seat, reached for her bag and stole a quick glance at her watch. Once she was home she would have a shower and wash her hair, then fix a simple dinner and have an early night. She sighed, finding re-assurance in this solitary, orderly programme. For one thing, it would help her recover from her shock.

They were almost there now. The cabbie was turning into the driveway and Carrie was reaching inside her bag for her wallet. But, midway, she stopped, her jaw dropping open, every muscle in her entire body turning to stone.

For parked beneath her balcony was a shiny black sports car, the hood down, exactly as it had been the other night. And walking towards her, looking quite jaunty, hands in pockets, was the very person she'd been hoping not to see.

CHAPTER FIVE

LEONE.

Carrie stared at him in horror for a moment, yet with a foolish sense of pleasure at just setting eyes on him again. He was dressed casually, in a pale suit with an open-neck shirt, his dark hair and tanned skin making a sharp, dramatic contrast, and that smile he was smiling was making her heart weep.

But now what should she do?

Her first instinct on catching sight of him had been to order the taxi driver to turn round and take her away. Hadn't she been thinking, just a moment ago, that she couldn't cope with seeing him? And the instant she'd laid eyes on him she'd known she'd been right. How could she possibly cope with this gorgeous creature now that she knew all the things she knew?

But it was too late to escape now. He was pulling the taxi door open. 'Hi,' he said. 'You're here at last.'

Carrie gritted her teeth. She would just have to do her best. She paid the taxi driver and reluctantly climbed out. 'Hi,' she said in response, wondering what on earth he wanted. Though she refrained from asking. That would only encourage him.

'I was sorry about today.' They were walking across the driveway. 'I hope Caterina explained to you that it couldn't be helped?'

'Yes.' Carrie felt a flicker of unease. Caterina had explained many things. Many things that might have been better left unexplained.

But she pushed these thoughts away. 'She was most informative,' she told him. 'And the dinner service was absolutely fabulous.'

'You liked it, did you?'

'I thought it was amazing.'

'Yes, it is pretty amazing.' He smiled. 'No doubt it'll provide an extra chapter for your book.'

'More than one, I suspect. I suspect two or three.' She already had a whole section devoted to it planned in her head! And she was confident now that it really would happen. After what Caterina had told her, she was perfectly sure of it.

She felt another twist inside her. Caterina had opened her eyes to many things. And that was the trouble. Eyes were sometimes best kept closed.

They had reached the foot of the stone steps and now Leone was turning to face her. 'So you've had a satisfying day,' he said. 'I'm glad.'

'It's been an excellent day.' Carrie suddenly felt awkward. Whatever he'd come for, she didn't want to know. The only thing she wanted was to make a rapid escape.

She feigned a stifled yawn. 'It's also been rather a long one. I'm just going off to have a shower and something to eat, and then I'm going to have an early night.'

And she turned away and started to climb the steps. That ought to send him on his way, she was thinking.

Rash hope.

'Oh, no, you're not.'

Leone was going nowhere. And neither was she, it seemed, for he had reached out and caught hold of her.

'You can have an early night some other night. Tonight you're dining with me.'

As his hand had grasped her arm, lightly but firmly holding her, Carrie's poor heart had almost shot out of her chest. She felt a rush of sensation, a delicious tingling from head to toe, and suddenly her legs felt like bales of straw beneath her.

She turned to look at him, blinking. I ought to be mad at him, she was thinking. He's got no right to grab me like this and tell me what to do! But as she looked at him and saw him smile it was quite impossible to feel angry—and quite impossible to do anything other than capitulate at once. For suddenly, in all the world there was nothing she wanted more than to have dinner with this quite shamelessly gorgeous man.

Like a fool she smiled back at him.

'OK,' she said.

Leone took her to a little place up in the hills behind the city.

'It's not very fancy,' he said as they were shown to a corner table with a plain rose-coloured cloth and a small vase of freesias. 'But the food's good and it's nice and private. No danger of paparazzi here.'

Carrie felt a chord strike within her. What he'd just said fitted perfectly with something his sister had told her this afternoon. But she said nothing for the moment. Perhaps she would bring all that up later.

She smiled across at him. 'I think it's perfect. I like places like this.' She glanced round approvingly at the dozen or so tables where none of the other diners was paying the least bit of attention to them. Then, as Leone handed her a menu, she suddenly remembered something—the long-running saga of her still unpaid debt to him!

She began to reach for her bag, which was slung over the back of her chair. 'You know, I've still never paid you that money I owe you. Let me do it now. I've got it here.'

'Right now? What will the waiters think if they see you handing me wads of money?' Leone threw her a wink and smiled across at her. 'Give it to me later. Anyway, there's no hurry.'

'Yes, there is. I've been wanting to give you it for ages.' But Carrie hesitated. A moment ago she'd been certain that no one was looking at them, but now it felt as though every eye in the entire place was on her.

She dropped her bag back. 'OK, I'll give it to you later.' In the car on the way home after their meal, she decided.

The food was simple but good. They had *gnocchi* with gorgonzola to start with—melt-in-the-mouth potato dumplings smothered with the famous cheese. Then they had chicken with garlic and a wonderful tomato salad. And when the waiter came to take their order for pudding Carrie wasn't at all certain if she could actually manage one, even though they all sounded quite wickedly tempting.

'Go on. Try the *crema di mascarpone*. It's delicious,' Leone urged her. 'I'm going to have some.'

So Carrie allowed herself to be persuaded and was glad that she had when the pudding arrived. This must surely be what heaven tastes like, she decided with a sigh as she took a mouthful of the creamy Marsala-laced concoction.

Finishing off the last spoonful, she sat back with a contented sigh. 'That was marvellous,' she told Leone. 'But before I go to bed I'll have to run at least ten laps round the garden to try and work some of those calories off!'

'You don't need to work off any calories. You're perfect as you are.'

'Flatterer!' Carrie laughed.

'That's not flattery. That's the truth.' His eyes were laughing back at her. 'You can't blame me for saying the truth.'

As their eyes met and held, Carrie felt a rush of pleasure. He was so easy to be with, such beguiling company—for she had enjoyed every minute of their dinner together. To be truthful, she had enjoyed it a little too much.

And that, of course, was what she'd been afraid of. For she'd known how hard it would be to resist him now that all her defences were gone.

Caterina had seen to that, she thought with a sense of helplessness. Caterina and all the stories she ought to have kept to herself.

Leone was asking her, 'Shall we have coffee now?'

Carrie nodded. 'OK.' She sat back in her chair. Perhaps, she was thinking as the waiter appeared at his elbow and Leone ordered two cups of espresso, it was time to confront him with what she'd discovered. For she knew she had to do it. She had to see how he reacted. His reaction would tell her how true it all was. For it was possible, after all, that Caterina had been exaggerating. She would be desperately grateful if that proved to be the case.

She laid her hands in her lap and looked across at him. 'Tell me something,' she said. 'About the other night. When those friends of yours requisitioned me and my friend's table...' She continued to look at him. 'Were you there when it actually happened?'

Leone looked back at her and smiled. 'Why do you ask?'

'I ask because I want to know. Were you?' she asked again.

'And why do you want to know?' He was enjoying teasing her. 'You never wanted to know before.'

No, she hadn't, quite simply because she'd assumed that he had been there. It had never occurred to her to assume anything else. At least, it hadn't until this afternoon.

Carrie sighed. This conversation could go on all evening and she still might not manage to get a straight answer out of him. A change of tactic was obviously called for.

She looked him straight in the eye. 'Your sister says she doesn't believe you were. I was telling her how we met—she was curious to know—and when I told her about the fiasco of the table she said, "Oh, that would never have happened if Leone had been there at the time."'

She paused and narrowed her eyes. 'According to your sister, pinching other people's restaurant tables in that high-handed manner isn't the sort of thing you go in for.' She sighed again. 'What I want to know is—was she right?'

'Do *you* think she was?'

He really was infuriating. 'I don't know what I think. At the time, when it happened, I assumed you were involved and you've never denied it.' She shrugged. 'So, maybe your sister's wrong, after all?'

'Maybe she is.'

'Why won't you tell me?' There was exasperation in Carrie's voice now. 'I really would rather like to know.'

Leone said nothing for a moment, just watched her across the table, the blue eyes seeming to study her very closely. Then he sat back in his seat and quietly told her, 'I arrived at the restaurant about ten minutes after the table fiasco. I was mad when I found out. That's why I came over to apologise.'

He continued to watch her. 'And Caterina was quite right. That's not the kind of behaviour I go in for or approve of.'

As Carrie looked at him she felt about half an inch high. She grimaced. 'I'm sorry.' Then she demanded in an accusing tone, 'But why didn't you tell me I'd got it all wrong?'

'You didn't ask. And I like people to make up their own minds about me. It's not for me to tell them what to think.'

'That's all very well—' Carrie's tone was suddenly sharp '—but how can people make up their minds if they don't know the facts?'

She felt angry, as though he had wilfully misled her. Though he hadn't, of course. She had misled herself.

Then she sank back in her seat. So Caterina had been right about that. She took a deep breath and braced herself to confront him with the rest.

'It seems I was wrong about you. And maybe on more counts than one.' She narrowed her hazel eyes. 'Caterina was telling me something else. She was telling me you have a full-time job.'

One jet-black eyebrow lifted. 'My, my,' he observed, 'it sounds as though my sister's been telling you a lot.' But his tone was light. He was more amused than annoyed.

'And is that true too? About the job, I mean?'

'Yes, of course it's true. And why do you look so surprised? Why on earth wouldn't I have a job?'

'Because you're the brother of the Duke. Because you're a count and all that. People like me tend to assume that people like you don't have jobs.'

'You think we're all idle pariahs? Surely that's a bit out of date? These are the 1990s we're living in. This isn't the last century.'

'Well, I didn't think *all* of you were idle par—'

Wishing she could bite off her tongue, Carrie let her voice trail off. Perhaps that wasn't the most diplomatic thing she could have said.

'I see. Just me?' To her surprise, Leone laughed. 'Well, maybe you got that idea because I like to keep my life private. It's not common knowledge that I have a nine-to-five job.' He smiled. 'Though some days eight-to-eight would really be more accurate.'

Carrie was staring down into her lap feeling even smaller than before. What Caterina had told her was all true and she had been totally wrong about him.

'He just wants to live his life, as far as possible, like an ordinary person,' Caterina had confided. 'Though, if you ask me, he works a hell of a lot harder than most people. He does his job as a member of the royal family, plus his other job as well.'

And now that she knew that to be true Carrie was left without defences. She could no longer disapprove of him as she had up until now. She could no longer tell herself he was a waster and a hooligan. Instead, to her dismay, she could only admire him.

She looked across at him now. There was one more thing, of course. In the course of their conversation Caterina had also insisted that the reports about his womanising were grossly exaggerated.

'He's no saint, of course. I wouldn't claim that. But he's not a woman-eater either. That's an invention of the Press. I don't know if he's ever been in love, but he's had a couple of longish relationships and I've always got the impression that he was totally faithful to his women.' She'd shrugged. 'I don't think you can expect any more of a single man than that.'

Carrie tended to agree, but was it true? she wondered. She let her eyes scan his face as the waiter brought their espressos. She could scarcely ask him that as well. It would begin to sound like a third degree. Besides, and more importantly, it would be a little revealing if she were to start demanding reassurances about his love life!

So she said nothing. She would reserve final judgement on that score and, in the meantime, give him the benefit of the doubt. For she had a strong gut feeling that his sister had been right about that too.

Which was disastrous news, of course. There wasn't a thing left to hold against him. Suddenly, she felt hopelessly, helplessly vulnerable.

They had their coffee and left the restaurant. And it was as they were climbing into the black car that Leone suggested, 'Let's go for a drive. I'd like to take you somewhere special. A secret spot I know with the most incredible view of the city.'

As she hesitated, he added, 'It's not far. Don't worry. I'll have you back home for the stroke of midnight.' And the next minute they were setting off up into the hills.

Driving through the darkened countryside in the open-top car would normally have been a thoroughly enjoyable experience, with the clean scent of the cypresses, the chatter of the cicadas, the carpet of stars spread out above their heads. But Carrie was still feeling tense. She shouldn't have agreed to this, she was thinking. This was the start of the slippery slope.

And she didn't want to fall. To fall for Leone would be disastrous. She was quite sure of that, though at this moment she couldn't think why.

At last they came to a stop on a high grassy knoll on the edge of a thicket of moon-dappled trees. And as Leone pulled on the handbrake Carrie sat forward in delight.

'This is incredible,' she gasped. 'You can see the entire city from here!'

For spread out below them was the most wonderful tapestry of city lights and shadowy, wooded hills, with the sea, off in the distance, gleaming like a mirror.

'Didn't I tell you this place was special?' Leone smiled at her obvious pleasure. 'And not everyone gets to come here. This is one of my secret places.'

'Well, I can see why. It's absolutely breathtaking.'

But a little too romantic, she was thinking. This was a spot for lovers. She could feel her heart begin to hammer. She should never have come with him to this secret, special place.

Leone had not suggested that they get out of the car, so Carrie didn't suggest it either. Maybe this was going to be brief. They would just admire the view and then go. So there was no point in getting out of the car and prolonging it.

But they weren't leaving just yet. Leone leaned back in his seat. 'I always find this place relaxing, especially at the end of a hard day. I often come up here just to unwind a bit,' he told her. 'And today, I'm afraid, has been that kind of day. It definitely calls for a bit of unwinding.'

Carrie's spine was pressed so hard against the leather back of the seat that she was in serious danger of popping out the other side. Unlike him, she didn't find this place relaxing in the least. On the contrary, it was tearing her poor nerves to shreds.

She said, struggling to sound cool, 'So it's been a hard day, has it?'

'It's been hectic. Nothing went smoothly. You know the kind of day? Appointments cancelled. People turning up late. The sort of day when you end up doing everything twice.'

He looked at her, noticing how she had edged away a little, and deliberately he sat back, widening the distance between them. He had no desire to make her nervous. That was the last thing on his mind.

Carrie picked up that move and its effect was most peculiar. Instead of feeling glad, she found herself feeling oddly disappointed. Perhaps she had nothing to worry about, after all.

She said, 'I had a good day. I got lots of things done: a few more interviews, some more research. I even managed to take a few more photographs. And, of course, seeing the dinner service was the perfect way to end it all.'

And as she said it she was thinking, Was all that really just today? She seemed to have lived at least two days in the space of one.

And the day wasn't even finished. She felt her stomach go tight. Perhaps it was better not to think about that.

Leone watched her as she spoke. 'I'm going to speak to Damiano again tomorrow. Though I doubt we'll be able to fix anything just at the moment. For one thing, right now he's up to his ears in work... And for another I won't be here. I've got to go to Paris on business tomorrow. I'll be away till the end of next week.'

'Oh, really?'

It was perfectly silly, but Carrie's heart plummeted to her shoes. A whole week without him! What a terrible prospect! Though she was mad to think such things. Utterly mad. What difference did it make to her even if he was gone for an entire month?

'But I promise I'll sort things out just as soon as I get back.' He looked at her. 'You don't mind waiting an extra week, I hope?'

'No, of course not. Not at all.' A week meant nothing to her, workwise. It was on a personal level that, in her foolishness, she was finding it such a blow.

'So, that's settled, then.'

Leone shifted in his seat. Perhaps, he was thinking, it's time to draw this excursion to a close. For she was still looking uneasy, her body stiff and forbidding. Clearly, she had little faith in his intentions.

He reached for the ignition key. 'I think we've seen the view now. I reckon it's time I drove you home.'

Carrie had already been feeling quite bereft, but she felt doubly bereft now. Was that it? Was it all over? Was she about to be packed off home now, without even a kiss to comfort her during the next lonely week?

It seemed too awful to bear. She turned sharply to face him—a little more sharply, indeed, than she had intended. 'Do we have to go just yet? I'm really in no hurry.'

And though one part of her cringed—that had sounded blatantly obvious—another, much larger part of her didn't care. On the contrary, she was quite shamelessly glad that she'd said it, for he had dropped his hand from the key and was turning to say to her, 'OK. If you like. I'm not in any hurry either.'

He had clearly read the signals wrong. Leone narrowed his eyes as he watched her. Women were so difficult to read sometimes, and this one especially. Though he had to confess that he had never met one he had wanted to read more.

A blush had touched her cheek, which simply made her more beautiful. He reached out one hand and touched her hair with his fingers, that wonderful honey-coloured hair, so thick and glossy, that felt like silk beneath his fingers.

He let his fingers trickle through it, noting the way she sighed and closed her eyes, and again he was struck by the same resemblance he'd seen before.

Smiling, he told her, 'You know, you look like an angel.'

Carrie turned round then to look at him. Was he joking? she was wondering. Was he making fun of her again?

She said, 'I must say no one's ever told me that before.'

Leone smiled. 'Ah, well, that's probably because most people aren't acquainted with the same angels I know.'

As he spoke, still touching her hair, he could feel a sudden softness in her. The tension had slackened. There was a lack of resistance.

He continued, 'There's an angel in our family chapel... Not a real angel, you understand. She's painted on the wall. And I noticed it the very first time I met you... It's amazing, but you look exactly like her.'

Carrie laughed. If he was making this up it was corny, but she liked it. And at least no one could accuse him of lacking imagination!

'I'll show her to you some time, for I can tell you don't believe me.' He smiled. 'She's always been my favourite angel.'

And as he said it he let his fingers slide to the back of her head and, moving closer, began to draw her towards him.

Carrie could feel her head spinning. Where he touched her she was burning. And every inch of her longed for the kiss that was about to happen. She sank against him with a small sigh and surrendered her lips to his.

It was less gentle than before. There was an urgency in his kiss this time. She could feel the fire in him reaching out to embrace her and she longed to fling herself recklessly onto the flames. To burn, exquisitely, on the glorious pyre of their shared passion.

His tongue flicked against her teeth, turning her stomach to ashes, and she could hear his breathing, as full of longing as her own.

'My beautiful angel!'

She pressed against him. 'Leone!'

For there was nothing in her head now but the heat of this moment. No thought whatsoever of all her previous doubts and worries. They had never existed, or, if they had, they had been mere madness. All that mattered was the thrilling reality of now.

One hand was on her breast, moulding the full contours, while with his other hand he was drawing her down lower in the seat, so that she was half sitting, half lying beneath him and she could feel the wonderful hard weight of him on top of her, the virile evidence of his desire pressing against her thighs.

Carrie caught her breath. What would happen if he tried to make love to her? Would she stop him? Would she resist? It wouldn't be easy. More than anything she longed to feel that hard muscle deep inside her.

He was unbuttoning her blouse. She began to unbutton his shirt, slipping her hand inside and pressing her palm against his chest. And the feel of it was thrilling. So warm and smooth and potent. Then she gasped as, with a tug at her bra, he released her breasts.

Carrie cried out. He had no mercy. He was strumming the hard nipples with his fingers, sending rockets of sensation ricocheting through her. Then, more merciless still, even as she whimpered he was bending down to take one blood-gorged peak in his mouth.

It was unbearable. She felt her fingers dig into his chest as the spiral of longing in her loins grew tighter. Any moment she would explode. The tension was unbearable. Never had any man taken her to such giddy heights before.

But just as she was thinking that she must either die or have him, right here, right this minute, or else lose her reason, he drew up and kissed her mouth and held her close for a moment.

'I think we ought to call a halt.' She could feel his body shivering. 'I want to make love to you, but not here, not like this,' he told her. He slipped her bra back into place and closed the front of her blouse. 'I want to do it properly, in a nice big bed, taking it slowly, with a whole night ahead of us. Not clumsily like this in the front seat of a car.'

He looked down at her, his hair tousled, a fierce look in his eyes. 'Believe me, that wasn't an easy decision. I've never wanted any woman so much in my life!'

Carrie clung to him, oddly grateful that he'd pulled them both back from the brink. She might have regretted it, though her body was aching for him still, just as she could feel that his still ached for hers.

She heard herself say, 'And I've never wanted any man so much.'

It seemed a reckless thing to say, but there was recklessness in the air. And she was glad that she'd said it as he smiled at her and told her, 'You're special to me, Carrie. I want you to know that.' He kissed her and held her. 'Very special indeed.'

They drove back to the villa in virtual silence. There simply seemed to be no need for words. It was as though something had been acknowledged, something basic, something vital. Something that now bound the two of them together.

At last they reached the villa and Leone told her, 'I'll phone you every day while I'm in Paris.' He kissed her, a kiss with fire, but achingly tender. 'And as soon as I get back I'll come and see you.'

'OK.'

Carrie was smiling. In a way, she dreaded his going, but at the same time she was filled with a wonderful new confidence. He *would* come back. She *would* see him again. And they *would* make love, just like he'd promised. Suddenly, the entire future felt gloriously bright.

'Look after yourself,' she told him. 'Have a safe journey.'

Then she was climbing up the steps to her apartment, glowing with a serene new happiness she had never known before.

*   *   *

Leone kept his promise to phone her every day. In fact, on quite a few days, he phoned her more than once.

'I'm missing you,' he'd tell her. 'It's miserable without you.'

And the words warmed Carrie's heart, for she was missing him too, dreadfully, more than she had ever known it possible to miss anyone. Every minute of every hour of every day she thought of him. It was a torture, but an exquisite one. He had become a part of her, it seemed.

For nothing had altered during his absence. That feeling of serene happiness had stayed in her heart. What will be will be, she told herself calmly. And this was obviously meant to be. There was no point in fighting it.

What did it matter if he was a count and she an ordinary working girl? She had thought that would be a barrier, but really it wasn't. When they were together, or when they spoke to one another on the phone, they were just two people, a man and a woman. And there was an affinity between them that she had felt with no man before. No, she and Leone had something special going.

At the end of the week came the phone call she'd been longing for.

'Everything's wrapped up,' Leone told her. 'I'll be flying home tomorrow on the afternoon flight.' He threw her a kiss down the line. 'Make sure you're ready and waiting for me. I'll come and see you straight from the airport.'

Carrie barely slept that night. The excitement was unbearable. But she didn't really care. If this was insomnia she didn't mind it, for lying thinking of tomorrow, and Leone, was sheer heaven.

She shivered beneath the sheets, her skin tingling with excitement. Tomorrow he would be here. At last they'd be together. She hugged herself with joy and pressed her face against the pillow. Tomorrow, finally, all her dreams would come true.

Leone hadn't slept much either, but for a rather different reason, one that he was regretting now as the plane touched down at San Rinaldo airport.

Last night should never have happened. It had been a foolish waste of time. And surely he didn't need to go in for that sort of nonsense now?

His little black sports car was waiting for him outside the arrivals hall, just as he'd arranged with Silvestro. He dumped his bags in the back and climbed into the driver's seat. Well, at least he'd escaped last night's folly intact, even though he was feeling a bit the worse for wear. And as soon as he saw Carrie he'd feel as good as new again.

He slipped the clutch into gear and headed for the highway. In just twenty minutes or so he would be with her. He felt a surge of pleasure. Carrie. Wonderful Carrie. He had thought about her constantly while he was away, a phenomenon that, frankly, had surprised him a little, for he had never been so obsessed with any woman before.

Nor had he ever missed any woman the way he had missed her. And missing her had been the hardest part to bear. But the waiting was almost over now. Soon she would be his.

But what Leone didn't know as he turned off the highway and headed up the winding, tree-lined road to the villa was that fate had a very different twist in store. For at that very moment Carrie was standing in her kitchen, sick to her soul, fighting back tears as she stared at the photograph on the front page of that morning's paper. Leone, in some Paris nightclub, embracing a half-naked blonde.

CHAPTER SIX

WHEN Leone arrived at Carrie's apartment he found the door firmly locked.

'What's going on? I know you're in there! Open up, Carrie! Let me in!' He beat at the door with his fists, a sudden panic inside him. 'What in heaven's name's going on? I'll knock the door down in a minute!'

Carrie sat slumped on the kitchen chair where she had sunk down in helpless misery, eyes still fixed on the photograph on the front page of the newspaper. She had conquered her tears and now she was struggling to slow down her breathing, which seemed to tear at her chest like a fistful of sharp daggers.

And as she sat there, barely aware of the banging on the door, her brain was shuttling about inside her head, struggling to bring some order to her current state of mental chaos. It was as though her world had crashed around her. She felt giddy and lost.

'Carrie! Open up!'

The banging was growing louder. Clenching her fists, Carrie stood up and breathed deeply for a moment. She was calm enough now, though her brain was still churning and the pain in her chest was like a great weight crushing her. But she would be able to deal with him now. She had finally got her mind straight. She knew now exactly what she must do.

Moving like an automaton, she picked up the newspaper, folded it carefully and tossed it in the bin. Then, slowly, feeling as though she was walking through deep water, she crossed the kitchen and went out into the hallway. And her hand hesitated for only a fraction of a second as she reached for the door-handle and pulled the door open.

'At last! What the hell's the matter? Why didn't you answer?'

At the sight of him Carrie very nearly burst into tears. I trusted him, she thought despairingly, and, just like that, he's betrayed me. The pain that tore inside her was too cruel to bear.

But she steeled herself and stifled it and looked into his face, struggling not to focus on those blue eyes that could melt her soul, on that mouth that could make her crazy, on that head of wild dark hair.

'Yes, I heard you,' she said. Her tone was as cold as marble. 'The reason I didn't answer was because I didn't want to see you.'

'You didn't want to see me?' He was pushing past her into the hall, taking her with him and closing the door behind them. 'I'm afraid you're going to have to explain what you mean by that,' he gritted.

Carrie had known it would not be easy, that he would refuse to be fobbed off. But she could be as wilful as he was and quite as determined. Nothing he could say or do could knock her off course.

She clenched her fists at her sides as he swung her round to face him, and told him in a voice that was as detached as her heart, 'I didn't want to see you because I want to end our relationship. I'm sorry, but that's the way it is.'

'Is it? Well, I'm sorry too, and you'll have to do better than that.' He was still holding her. 'What brought about this sudden change of mind?'

'It wasn't particularly sudden.' She pulled herself free of him, coldly, as though she found physical contact with him distasteful. 'I've been doing some thinking this past week and I've realised I don't really care for you. It was just a silly flirtation, but now the flirtation is over.'

'I see. It was just a silly flirtation, was it?'

Leone stood back and regarded her through narrowed eyes—eyes that really were the perfect blue of lapis lazuli, Carrie thought miserably. Then she pushed that thought away. They were the faithless eyes of a betrayer.

He continued to watch her. 'Well, I must say,' he pointed out, 'that definitely wasn't the impression I got in the course of our numerous phone calls this week. On the contrary, the impression I got was very different. I got the impression you cared for me as much as I care for you.'

How could he say such a thing? Anger tore at Carrie's heart. He wasn't just faithless, he was an out-and-out liar. He didn't care for her. All he cared about were his sexual conquests.

She wanted to throw that in his face, to tell him she knew the truth, to shame him—if he was capable of shame—with the proof of his vileness. But that would be the wrong thing to do. He would only try to lie his way out of it, and she, in her foolishness, might end up believing him. And that would only lead to more pain in the future.

No, it would be much better by far just to stick to her own lie and put an end to this miserable travesty right now.

She drew herself up. 'I was simply being courteous. There are certain things one shouldn't do over the phone—and in my book one of them is end a relationship. That's something that ought to be done face to face.'

For the first time he smiled, though it was a smile with little humour. The wide mouth curled at the corners, but the blue eyes remained hard.

'So, you were being courteous, were you?' His tone was mocking. 'Personally, I would have said you went way beyond courtesy. But maybe I'm mistaken. Maybe you say these things to everyone, just to be kind.'

Carrie could not hide a blush. She glanced down quickly at the floor, feeling a sudden sharp stab of misery inside her. Yes, she had said some things that would have been hard to describe as courteous—like how desperately she missed him and how she thought of him all the time.

She kept her eyes fixed on the floor. 'Perhaps I shouldn't have said those things. I can only apologise if I misled you.'

Leone laughed a scornful laugh. 'You can only apologise if you misled me?' Then he reached out suddenly to catch her chin with his fingers, jerking her face up none too gently, forcing her to look at him. 'You're misleading me all right. But were you misleading me then or are you misleading me now?' His tone was as harsh as rough stone against metal. 'I'm sorry, but there's something here that just doesn't ring right.'

The way he was holding her he was hurting her. His fingers were like steel bands, digging into her flesh, threatening to crush the bone beneath. But though Carrie winced it wasn't the pain she was principally aware of, but the treacherous way her heart had jumped when he had taken hold of her, and the way, even now, that her blood was rushing inside her at the cruelly intoxicating touch of his flesh.

It was crazy, but she longed to sink against his hand and feel that fierce pressure turn into a caress. To tell him she had been lying, that she didn't mean a word of what she'd just told him, that she cared for him with all her heart, as she had cared for no man before. And it was the hardest thing in the world to know that she must say none of those things. Tears tore at her throat. With a shivering sigh she closed her eyes.

And then, in a measured tone, she heard herself demanding, 'What's wrong with you? Why can't you just accept what I'm saying? I don't want to see you any more. It's perfectly straightforward. There's really no point in discussing it endlessly.'

She opened her eyes again. 'And kindly let go of my face.'

If she had opened her eyes just a fraction of a second later she would have missed the look that flashed across his face. It was a look she could not quite fathom, but which had an intensity that made her breath catch. It was probably anger, she decided. It couldn't possibly be hurt. The only part of him likely to be hurt was his vanity.

His hand had dropped from her face and he was taking a step away from her. 'You're right. There's no point in discussing this any further. I'm sure we

both have far better things to do.' And with that he
started to turn towards the door.

But there was still one more thing.

'Just a minute,' Carrie told him. Then she darted
through to the kitchen and grabbed her bag, which
lay on the table. A moment later she re-emerged
clutching some folded banknotes in her hand. 'This
is the money I owe you,' she told him, holding them
out to him.

Leone had opened the front door and was already
halfway outside. And for a moment he frowned as
though he didn't understand. He had entirely forgotten about the restaurant-bill money.

When he didn't move, Carrie marched up to him
and thrust the money at him. 'There,' she said
brittlely. 'Finally, we're even. I think that closes the
books between us.'

Leone said nothing, just pushed the money into his
shirt pocket, turned on his heel and hurried down the
stone stairs. Then, without a backward glance, he
climbed into his car and, with a sharp squeal of tyres,
drove away.

Carrie watched from the doorway. 'Good rid-
dance!' she declared angrily. 'I hope I never see you
again!'

Then she slammed the door shut and burst
into tears.

Carrie's misery was real enough, but it didn't take her
long to realise that, really, she ought to be grateful
for what had happened. Leone had lied to her and
made a fool of her and betrayed her totally, but there
was this much to be grateful for—that she had found

out in time exactly what kind of despicable man he was.

For he was, after all, in spite of his sister's assurances to the contrary, the very type of man she had believed him to be in the beginning. A faithless Lothario incapable of keeping his zip shut. The type of man she wanted absolutely nothing to do with.

But how he had taken her in! How nearly she had been seduced!

All that flim-flam about the angel on the wall of the family chapel. He probably fed that corny line to every girl he met! And the way he had taken her on a drive to one of his supposedly secret places, pretending to share it with her because she was special . . . well, that was a laugh! He probably took all his women there! Hadn't she herself thought it was a perfect spot for seduction?

She felt a knife inside her. And it had certainly worked with her.

But at least it was over now, and she had done the right thing. There was no place in her life for a man like Leone, the handsome, exciting, faithless playboy count. She'd been saved from the most reckless folly of her life.

But, though she tried to feel glad about her lucky escape, all she was aware of was the wretched gnawing ache in her heart.

The phone call came as she was having breakfast a couple of days later.

'This is the Duke's office,' the voice at the other end told her, almost causing Carrie to drop the receiver in shock. 'You are invited to dinner with the

Duke and Duchess, along with a group of other guests, at the Palazzo Verde this evening. Dress is informal and a car will be sent to pick you up at eight o'clock.'

Carrie hung up, feeling quite dazed. This was the last thing she'd been expecting—that Leone would keep his promise to arrange a meeting for her with his brother. Over the past couple of days she'd been toying with the idea of resurrecting her plan to approach the palace press office again herself. She'd been quite sure that there was scant likelihood of Leone delivering the goods now.

Though perhaps it hadn't been Leone. Perhaps it had been Caterina. Yes, Carrie decided, that was much more likely. She must make a point of thanking Caterina for her intervention.

But first things first. She rushed through to her bedroom and flung open her wardrobe with a cry of despair. Informal dress, she suspected, did not mean T-shirt and jeans. More likely, what it meant was a short cocktail dress rather than a ballgown, no tiara required and only one's second-best diamonds. And though she could fulfil the tiara requirement with no trouble at all she didn't possess a single dress that would be even remotely suitable.

'Oh, Lord,' she moaned despairingly. 'I don't have a thing to wear!'

By a stroke of good fortune she had no appointments that morning. She'd been planning to spend the day transcribing some of her taped interviews. But that could wait, she decided as she got dressed and called a cab. First, she had a bit of serious shopping to do!

It was an exquisite kind of torture, searching for a suitable outfit.

In the end, sticking to her belief that simple was usually what worked best, she opted for an elegant off-the-shoulder blue silk dress with delicious hand-worked beading around the sleeves and neck. It cost a fortune, but it looked fabulous and it was so well made it would last for ever. And it would go perfectly with her navy shoes and bag.

There was only one thing troubling her. Would Leone be at the dinner tonight? She prayed that he would not, though her prayers were probably not necessary. She'd never heard from him again and he was unlikely to want to seek out her company. No, Leone, she felt certain, would have better things to do tonight.

So it was in a highly positive frame of mind that, watched by an increasingly bedazzled Signora Rossi, Carrie climbed into the ducal car at eight o'clock sharp. Finally, she was going to meet the Duke and get permission to use the dinner service in her book!

Carrie was met at the palace doorway, as usual, by Flavia, and this time she was greeted almost like an old friend.

'How nice to see you again. And what a beautiful dress!'

Then she was led along corridors, up stairs and under archways to a part of the palace where she had never been before. And suddenly, to her very fingertips, she was buzzing with excitement. Who would ever have dreamed of this?

She knew they were nearly there when they turned into a blue-carpeted corridor, for suddenly Carrie

could hear the sounds of voices and laughter. She felt
herself tense a little. This was it! she was thinking.
Then she was being shown into a room hung with
glittering chandeliers where fifty or so people were
standing drinking and talking. And she had been absolutely right in her interpretation of 'informal'. The
women were all in short dresses and there wasn't a
tiara in sight!

Flavia escorted her to one of the groups and introduced her while a waiter brought her a tall glass
of champagne. Then Flavia disappeared and Carrie
had a sudden rush of panic as she realised she was on
her own amongst this crowd of elegant strangers.
Though she really needn't have worried. She was able
to join in the conversation quite easily. Like herself,
most of the people in the group were visitors to the
country and the talk was mainly about how much they
were all enjoying San Rinaldo.

She was just starting to get involved when a voice
exclaimed at her elbow, 'Ah, there you are! It's good
to see you!'

Carrie turned round with a smile. 'It's good to see
you too.' She grinned at Caterina, who was looking
quite splendid in a red silk dress. 'I'm really pleased
to have been invited here tonight.'

With a polite nod to the rest of the group, Caterina
slipped an arm through Carrie's and drew her aside
as she proceeded to tell her, 'Damiano frequently has
these little dinners, just to welcome various visitors
to the country. They're usually quite enjoyable, though alas I won't be able to stay long at
this one.' She gave a conspiratorial wink. 'I have
another appointment.'

Carrie understood immediately. Over tea that
afternoon Caterina had told her about the wonderful
man she was in love with. Carrie smiled back at her
now. 'Good for you,' she told her, happy that her
friend's romance was clearly flourishing. Though she
couldn't quite stifle a sudden thrust of personal
misery. There'd be no such amorous pleasures on the
menu for her.

'I think we're making a move at last.'

Caterina's gaze had shifted to the tall double doors
at the end of the room which a pair of gold-liveried
footmen were at that moment pulling open.

'What happens now,' she explained, 'is that we all
file into the dining room in pairs. Then, once we're
all seated, Damiano and Sofia will appear. By the way,
it's been arranged that you'll see Damiano after
dinner—'

She broke off and glanced round her. 'I'd better go
and join the Finnish ambassador—he's my escort for
the evening.' She craned her neck. 'Ah, there he is,'
she said, waving to a handsome blond man. Then she
gave Carrie's arm a squeeze. 'Enjoy the meal,' she
told her. 'Bye for now. I'll see you again.'

Then she was dashing off into the crowd, which
was already forming itself into pairs, leaving Carrie
wondering what on earth she was supposed to do next.

I don't have an escort, she was thinking in panic.
I'm going to have to walk in there alone!

But then, making her jump, a cool hand suddenly
touched her arm and a voice said, 'Allow me to escort
you to your place.'

Carrie whirled round, her heart stopping, and found herself looking into a pair of long-lashed eyes the perfect blue of lapis lazuli.

Hot colour flew to her cheeks. 'What are you doing here?' she gasped.

'I've come to escort you in to dinner.' Leone held out his arm to her. Then, as she hesitated, he took her arm and slipped it through for her, exactly as he'd done the other evening. 'Let's not keep everyone waiting,' he admonished her in a light tone.

Carrie could think of nothing to say. She didn't even know what she was thinking. She felt quite stunned, totally confused and foolishly grateful to see him— none of which added up to any sort of coherent frame of mind. So, she just stayed silent and allowed herself to be led through the double doors and into the spectacular crimson and gold dining room.

It was a room to make your mouth water, even before you got to the food! Lush silk draperies adorned the tall windows, chandeliers the size of Colorado blazed from the ceiling and priceless Rembrandts and Titians hung from the walls. But what dominated the room was the mile-long mahogany table, set with glistening French crystal, antique English silver and wonderful gold-leaf-decorated Castello porcelain. Though what Carrie was principally aware of as she stepped into this wonderland was the tall man at her side, dressed in an immaculate dark suit, whose nearness was turning her insides to powder.

He led her to their places and they sat down together, though Carrie hadn't dared even to slip him a glance. What was going on? Why on earth had he turned up like this? Her brain was going round in circles.

She waited till her frantic heart had calmed down a little, then she half turned towards him, though not looking him fully in the face.

'Why are you subjecting me to this?' she demanded in a tight tone. 'I thought I told you I never wanted to see you again.'

'I couldn't let you dine unescorted. That would have been most unchivalrous. Especially since I'm responsible for you being here tonight.'

'You mean *you* set it up?'

'Why so surprised?' Black eyebrows lifted. 'Didn't I say I would fix it for you to meet my brother? What's the matter? Do you think everyone's as fickle as you are?'

'That's a good one!'

Carrie did turn round then, her eyes blazing with indignation at the sheer hypocrisy of that remark. And she was surprised to see that he was smiling.

'Yes,' he purred, 'I thought that would get a reaction.'

Carrie was continuing to glare at him, but already she was suspicious. There was something far too easy about his demeanour. It was as though that last little spat between them had never happened. For there was no rancour about him—as she would have expected. Either she hadn't even hurt his vanity or something else was going on.

And then he enlightened her. 'I know why you were mad at me. You saw that photograph. The one in the paper.'

Carrie felt her insides twist. It would be senseless to deny it. So she told him, 'Yes, I saw the photograph.' Though she hurried on to assure him, 'But the photograph wasn't important. I meant the things I said.'

She must reaffirm the lie that had served her so well before, the lie that she simply cared nothing for him.

To her dismay, he just smiled. He wasn't buying her lie this time.

'Liar,' he told her. 'You didn't mean them at all. You were jealous, that's all. And it was perfectly understandable. But don't worry, I have a perfectly good explanation for everything. We can be back where we left off in no time at all.'

What a presumption! 'Oh, no, we can't! We won't be getting back anywhere. So you can forget about wasting time with explanations. I don't even want to hear them, and I wouldn't believe them if I did!'

'We'll see. I think otherwise. In fact, I'm sure of it.' The blue eyes poured into hers for a moment and suddenly his tone was deadly serious as he added, 'I won't let you leave here until you've heard me out and I've convinced you. Take my word for it, for that's a promise.'

Panic rose up inside her. This was precisely what she'd been afraid of—that he would insist on explaining things and she might end up believing him!

'No!' she protested. She must not let it happen! She shook her head at him. 'You'll never convince me!'

'Oh, yes, I will,' he asserted, still in that grim tone. Then he smiled. 'I can see this is going to be an interesting evening.'

And it was at that moment that the Duke and Duchess appeared.

Everyone around the vast table was rising to his or her feet. Carrie and Leone rose too as the royal couple proceeded to their seats. And, as she watched them, just for a moment Carrie forgot about Leone, the handsome, faithless thorn in her side.

It was Damiano who held her eye. He was a spectacular-looking man—though she already knew that from the pictures she had seen of him. A few years older than Leone, he was as tall as his brother, with the same jet-black hair, though his was sleek and straight, and with eyes as dark as whirlpools and as piercing as sabres.

He had a wonderful carriage, regal and commanding. In fact, everything about him was commanding and regal. There was none of the informality that was part of Leone's attraction, and there was a seriousness about him that his brother mostly lacked. He was a man to be reckoned with. Intriguing and a little daunting. Carrie frowned and found her gaze drifting curiously to Sofia.

Oh, yes, she was beautiful. Even more beautiful than her photographs, with wonderful red-gold hair and a pale oval face. In the sapphire dress she was wearing the bump of her pregnancy barely showed and there was a gentleness and an innocence about her that was exceedingly touching. But Caterina had been right. There was something amiss. Behind the serene, regal smile she did not look happy.

The Duke and Duchess took their seats and with a shuffle everyone sat down. And, abruptly, Carrie found herself jolted back to the prickly present—namely Leone and his threats to convince her with his lies. That threatened to ruin her entire evening.

At the moment, as etiquette demanded, he was chatting to the woman on his other side. Good, Carrie thought, he can speak to her all evening. I'll strike up a conversation with the man next to me. She half turned, inclining towards him, about to put her plan into action, when at that very moment strong fingers closed around her wrist.

'What I was speaking about earlier... This is neither the time nor the place. You and I will have our little chat after dinner.' As she whirled round to look at him and indignantly snatched her hand away Leone smiled and added, 'And remember what I told you... You won't be leaving here until I've convinced you.'

Carrie didn't bother to protest. He would never convince her and the little talk he was threatening her with would never happen anyway. Caterina had told her she'd be meeting the Duke after dinner. And after that she would make a hasty escape.

The dinner, however, Carrie wouldn't have missed for anything. Course after glorious course—she lost count after the fifth one!—and each dish more mouth-watering than the one before it. Salmon, partridge, all kinds of vegetables and salads, soufflés, cheeses and three kinds of pudding. Carrie had never eaten so luxuriously, nor so copiously, in her life.

Even Leone didn't spoil things. His behaviour was exemplary. When he wasn't chatting to his other neighbour and Carrie wasn't chatting to hers he made her laugh with anecdotes about his cars and his childhood and intrigued her with stories about his travels round the world. It was rather sad, Carrie reflected, that he could be so utterly charming, such exceptionally good company, so hopelessly attractive, and yet, underneath it all, such a faithless rotter.

But she didn't dwell on that. She just concentrated on enjoying herself. Which wasn't in the least hard. It was a magical evening.

There was only one slightly jarring note and probably only Carrie noticed it. Her eye was suddenly caught by Caterina across the table politely taking her leave of the Finnish ambassador. And as she watched her she smiled. Clearly, she was off to meet her lover.

But then for some reason Carrie's eye was drawn to the Duke, who was also watching Caterina's departure, but with such a black look on his face that Carrie felt herself shiver. Either he was angry at her leaving early or he disapproved of where she was going. Intuitively, Carrie sensed that the latter was more likely.

For Caterina had told her that her brother did not approve of her current romance. Her lover was a commoner and the Duke considered him unsuitable. Apparently, they'd exchanged angry words on the subject.

Carrie watched her as she left the room with that confident, no-nonsense stride she had and she couldn't help smiling a little to herself. Whether her brother approved or not, Caterina would go her own way. She wasn't the sort of girl to be told what to do!

The dinner drew to a close and people began to leave the table and drift into the drawing room for coffee and brandy.

This is it, Carrie was thinking. This is when the Duke's supposed to see me. She stole a quick glance at Leone who was exchanging a word with his other neighbour. So long, it's goodbye time, she told his oblivious back. You can keep your phoney explanations for your more gullible girlfriends. And she slipped quietly from her chair and began to head for the drawing room.

But she never actually made it. Before she knew what was happening, an arm was round her waist and she was being steered in the opposite direction.

She squirmed furiously to free herself. 'What the devil do you think you're doing? I have an appointment with your brother!'

But her protests were a waste of breath. Suddenly, she was being propelled through a side door, then across a little ante-room, where a couple of waiters blinked but said nothing, then down a narrow passageway and into a small sitting room which was in total darkness until Leone switched the light on.

Then she was being plonked down in a chair and he was turning the key in the lock, then pocketing it with a triumphant little smile as he told her, 'Now you and I are going to have our little talk.'

CHAPTER SEVEN

CARRIE was almost speechless with fury.

Almost, but not quite.

She sprang to her feet. 'This is outrageous! I have an appointment with your brother!' Her eyes blazed at her captor. 'Let me out of here this instant!'

'I shall let you out when I've finished with you.' Leone regarded her without mercy. 'And how long that takes depends entirely on you.'

He was mad! He was a sadist! He had no conscience whatsoever! He really did intend to keep her a prisoner here and force her to listen to all his lies and excuses!

Carrie took a step towards him, fists clenched, eyes flashing, resisting only with difficulty the urge to take a whack at him. Physical contact, she sensed, would not be a good idea.

She spat at him through clenched teeth, 'You're wasting your time, you know. I'm not interested in hearing what you have to tell me. Like I already told you, I don't want anything to do with you. Nothing you can say is going to alter that.'

'We'll see.' Leone smiled down at her, then he took a step away from her and seated himself with an unhurried air on one of the gilt-framed tapestry chairs behind him. 'First, I'd like you to hear my side of the story.'

'But not now!' Carrie let out a wail of frustration. 'I have to see your brother now! Caterina told me it's been arranged that I speak to him after dinner!'

'Yes, I know that. I arranged it. Why don't you sit down?'

'I don't want to sit down! I want to go and keep my appointment!' Carrie was almost weeping with misery. 'Why are you doing this to me? It's not fair! This is important to me! Why are you behaving like a rotten bully?'

This stream of angry invective had about as much effect on him as a poke in the ribs with a stick of limp celery.

Leone smiled. 'Calm down. You won't miss your appointment. I arranged with my brother that I'd take you to him after coffee. So we have plenty of time. At least another twenty minutes.'

Carrie felt a rush of relief, followed instantly by suspicion. 'Do you mean that?' She peered into his face for signs of treachery. 'Is that the truth? You're not lying to me, are you?'

'Why do you always assume I'm lying?' He peered back at her, the blue eyes narrowing accusingly. 'It seems to me that you're the one who goes in for lying. Omitting to tell me you'd seen that photograph in the newspaper, for example. That was a lie, you know. A lie of omission.'

'And I suppose you haven't lied to me?'

'Not that I'm aware of.'

Carrie laughed a scoffing laugh. 'That's a lie in itself.' She could have offered him a list of the lies he'd told her—the one about her being special to him coming top of the list!

Then, before he could protest, she plonked herself down at her chair again and folded her arms across her chest. 'Oh, well, I suppose I don't really have much choice but to sit here and listen to you reeling off some more.'

She'd just have to trust him, she decided, on the issue of her appointment with the Duke. And if that turned out to be a lie too she'd have his head on a stick!

'Good. I have your attention at last.' Leone leaned forward in his seat. 'Now just try not to interrupt and listen to what I have to say...'

Carrie regarded him sceptically. OK, I won't say a word, she was thinking. But that doesn't mean I'm going to swallow what you're about to tell me! And she kept her arms firmly folded across her chest.

'OK, let me explain what actually happened on that last night in Paris when the photograph was taken...' He leaned his elbows on his thighs, letting his hands fall between his knees. 'After we'd concluded our business my French associates insisted on taking me out for a celebration. I thought it was only going to be dinner, but they insisted on going on to a nightclub afterwards and, though I wasn't really in the mood, I went along with them.'

He paused. 'It was unlike me not to be in the mood. Normally, I confess, I quite enjoy that sort of thing. But nightclubbing was the last thing on my mind that evening. All I was thinking about was you and getting back here to you as soon as possible...'

As he looked deep into her eyes Carrie felt herself flush. She hadn't expected that and it had twisted something deep inside her. In spite of her mood of scepticism, she found herself wishing it might be true.

Leone was continuing, 'We went to a place near Montmartre, and we'd scarcely sat down when one of my hosts insisted on inviting some girls to join our table.' He made a face of distaste that looked remarkably genuine, though Carrie suspected he was probably pretty well practised at looking genuine. 'They were girls of a certain type. Well, you saw the one in the photograph. And before I knew it that blonde with the plunging neckline was all over me.'

He made another face. 'Believe me, I made a rapid escape. I just finished my drink and made an excuse that I had to leave. So that photographer must have been quick—and I had no idea he'd taken a picture. And I might never have known if Caterina hadn't pointed it out to me, right there on the front page of next morning's paper.'

He sighed. 'I reckon I'm used to this sort of thing. The Press seem to think they have every right in the world to take pictures like that just in order to sell newspapers. And usually it doesn't bother me. It's just part of the package. But this time was different . . .' There was a pained look in his eyes. 'This time it mattered because it screwed things up between you and me.'

Carrie had known this would happen. She sat there helplessly, feeling all her fine scepticism dribble away. She was not entirely convinced, but the truth was that she wanted to be.

Quite unconsciously, she unfolded her arms from her chest and let her hands drop to clasp each other lightly in her lap.

He was continuing, 'If you knew how much I care about you, Carrie, you could never have doubted me. This would never have happened.'

Then he paused and held her eyes with a look of such entreaty that Carrie felt her poor confused heart tilt over. 'Believe me, I could never even look at another woman now. That's just not in my mind. Don't you know I'm quite besotted with you? And that photograph was just a nonsense. It didn't mean a thing.'

He frowned at her. 'But why on earth didn't you tell me you'd seen it?'

'I don't know. I was too hurt, too angry, I guess. I just wanted to finish with you. I didn't want to discuss it.'

She looked into his face, into the wonderful lapis eyes, and it seemed that every inch of her entire being was aching. Aching to believe him. Aching for his words to be the truth. For she was still a little afraid to accept his story totally.

She believed the bit about the nightclub. Well, ninety-nine per cent she did. But the rest—what he felt for her—had he really meant that? Men often said such things to women. Maybe he'd just said it to appease her? She felt tied up knots. She hadn't expected any of this.

'I'm sorry it happened.' Leone was still watching her. 'You'd every right in the world to be upset.' He drew his chair closer to her. 'But you do accept my explanation don't you? Tell me you do, Carrie. Tell me you believe me.' And as he said it he reached out and took hold of her hand and clasped it firmly between the two of his.

Dear heavens, this was terrible. Her heart was tripping inside her. She held her breath. 'I don't disbelieve you,' she said at last.

She was scared to say more than that. She had to keep something in reserve, just in case it all proved to be a total fabrication.

Leone squeezed her hand and smiled. 'Well, at least that's progress. And I guess I'll just have to make do with that for now.' He glanced at his watch, then raised her fingers and kissed them. 'It's time I took you to see my brother. We mustn't have you missing that appointment. Come on.'

He stood up, drawing her with him, bending to plant a warm kiss on her forehead. Then, still holding her hand, he led her towards the door.

Heart beating, still confused, Carrie followed him without a word.

The meeting with the Duke couldn't have gone better.

He was perfectly charming to her, though a little forbidding—which was just his manner, Carrie decided. There was no doubt at all that he possessed a streak of ruthlessness but she could see a kind of warmth too in the midnight-black eyes. He would make an uncompromising enemy, but a good and true friend. And, above all, he would be fair. He was the sort of man you could depend on.

But most important, as far as she was concerned, he was in favour of her project.

'I'll be happy for you to include the dinner service in your book,' he had told her as the three of them sat drinking brandy from crystal balloons—for Sofia had already disappeared off to her rooms and Carrie and Leone and the Duke had retired to a small ante-room away from the other guests.

'Naturally,' he had continued, 'I shall require you to be accompanied at all times while you're taking photographs or examining the pieces. And I shall also need to vet both photographs and text before any of it is actually published.' He had smiled at her. 'Are you agreeable to these conditions?'

'Oh, perfectly.' They were no more than Carrie would have expected. 'And thank you,' she had added. 'I'm really grateful for this opportunity. And I promise you won't be disappointed with the treatment the service receives.'

The Duke had nodded and smiled knowingly. 'No, I'm sure I won't. You see, I've already taken the trouble to acquaint myself with your previous work— on which I must congratulate you. I found it most impressive. I can see that the collection will be in highly professional hands.'

After the meeting was over, Leone had suggested to Carrie that the two of them take a walk in the palace gardens. And that was where they were now, me-andering hand in hand between moon-dappled flowerbeds and topiaried hedges, chatting and drinking in the cool night air, skirting the huge lawn where a pair of peacocks strolled.

'Well, you made a good impression there.' Leone lifted her hand and kissed it. 'I think my brother was extremely impressed with you.' He looked into her eyes and smiled. 'Though not half as impressed as me, of course.'

Carrie had to suppress a shiver at the touch of his lips against her fingers. He was making all the little hairs on the back of her neck stand up.

She smiled back at him and pulled a face. 'If he was impressed, it was thanks to you. You seem to have done a pretty thorough PR job on me.'

For it had been perfectly clear that the Duke had come to the meeting already virtually convinced that he would give her the go-ahead. As he had said himself, he valued Leone's opinion and Leone had had nothing but unconditional praise for her—for her personal integrity and for her professionalism.

She laughed. 'All I had to do was try and live up to what you'd told him.'

'I'd only told him the truth. But don't kid yourself,' Leone added. 'If my brother hadn't been impressed with you he would never have given the go-ahead. In the end, Damiano always makes up his mind for himself.'

Yes, that would be true. But all the same Carrie felt grateful for the way Leone had prepared the way for her. Though it was a mixed kind of gratitude. He was undermining her resistance. Over the past hour or so—first with his brother, then here in the garden— there had been an easiness between them, as though they had never fallen out, as though there had never been an angry word between them. And she still wasn't sure if that was what ought to be happening.

But she tried to keep her mind off that, at least for the moment. She said, 'I liked your brother. I thought he was pretty impressive too.'

'He is pretty impressive. And he does a great job.' Leone was leading them towards one of the marble fountains whose splashing water sparkled like liquid pearls in the moonlight. He shook his head. 'But I wouldn't be in his shoes for anything.'

There was a stone bench in front of the fountain. As they sat down on it together, Carrie turned round to glance at him curiously. 'Why do you say that?' she wanted to know.

'My brother's life, from dawn to dusk, is consumed with affairs of state. It's virtually impossible for him to have any private life at all. That wouldn't suit me. I've always been very glad that I was born the second son and not the first.' He smiled. 'And very glad now that I probably won't be heir to the throne much longer. Believe me, I'm keeping my fingers crossed that Sofia gives birth to a boy.'

He turned to her. 'Don't get me wrong. I don't begrudge doing my duty. I love my country. There's no two ways about that. But I'm not like Damiano. With Damiano it's an obsession. For Damiano, his duty to his country comes first, second and last.'

Carrie found that easy to believe. Hadn't she seen for herself the intensity that glowed at the back of the midnight eyes? And she found herself thinking for a moment of Sofia and wondering if this explained a little of the girl's sadness. Did the Duke perhaps neglect his beautiful young wife?

Leone was continuing. 'Caterina and I are different. Perhaps we have a broader view of life. At any rate . . .' he smiled ' . . . I've always been very glad that it didn't fall to me to be the ruler of my country. I'm much happier messing about with my cars.'

He turned to look at her and kissed her hand again. 'You must come to the workshop some time and see where I work. That is,' he added, 'if it would interest you.'

'I'd love to come.' It would interest her greatly, she was thinking. For suddenly she felt hungry to know more about him. To see inside his head. To understand what made him tick. Finally, to sort out the puzzle that was Leone.

One thing she knew was that she had misjudged him badly.

She'd done it right from the start, from their first meeting in the restaurant, and had continued to do so in stops and starts ever since.

Take the business of the photograph. It hadn't even occurred to her that there might be a perfectly innocent explanation. And with no trouble at all she had jumped to the conclusion that all the things he'd said to her that evening in the car had been barefaced lies, cynical invention. And maybe it was the moonlight, or simply his nearness, or the distracting way he kept kissing her hand, but suddenly she was convinced that she'd been desperately unfair to him. He was really none of the things she kept accusing him of at all.

While she'd been thinking all this, Leone had been watching her closely, as though he too was trying to figure something out. He said now, kissing her hand again, 'I want to show you something.' He started to stand up. 'Come on.' He took her hand.

Carrie didn't ask what it was. She knew he wouldn't tell her, and anyway she rather fancied the idea of a surprise. She just allowed him to lead her along the broad gravel path that skirted the west wing of the palace, past the lake where a pair of swans silently glided, their backs as soft as thistledown in the starlight.

But though she asked no questions she was growing curiouser by the minute as they turned onto a narrow stone-flagged path that curved between a low-slung canopy of trees. And then, as they turned the corner, she had her first major clue.

The low building in front of them, with its curved Gothic doorway, narrow stained-glass windows and air of having been there for ever, was obviously the family chapel. But Carrie still didn't say anything, though she had a strong suspicion now that she knew what he was about to show her. And suddenly her heart had quickened in her breast.

The only light inside the chapel was from the flickering candles that cast a warm yellow glow over the ancient frescoed walls. Leone took her hand more firmly and led her to the altar, pointing to the painting on the frieze behind it.

'Look there,' he told her. 'What do you see?'

Carrie peered where he was pointing, eyes squinting against the semi-darkness, trying to make out the painted figures on the wall. And she was just about to shake her head and tell him it was too dark to make out anything when suddenly something clicked and she could see her perfectly.

'It's your angel!' she gasped. 'The one you told me about!'

For there she was in all her glory, with her golden wings and flowing robes, and even Carrie could see that the resemblance was uncanny. The angel's features were almost identical to her own. It gave her the strangest sensation in the pit of her stomach.

'Isn't she beautiful?' Leone was standing behind her, his hand lightly on her waist as he gazed up at the angel too. 'I've spent hours looking at that angel in the course of my life. I first fell in love with her when I was about ten years old. I used to dream of meeting her, but I never thought I would.'

He seemed to hold his breath for an instant. 'At least, I thought that till I met you.'

Quite spontaneously, without thinking what she was doing, Carrie reached up and laid her hand softly over his. What a lovely thing to say. She felt deeply moved by his words. No one had ever paid her such a very special compliment before.

She waited till they were outside again, heading back down the stone-flagged path, then she turned to him and told him what was truly in her heart.

'All the things you told me tonight...your explanation about the photograph... I believe you. I believe you without reservation.' She looked deep into his eyes. 'And I'm really sorry I ever doubted you.'

'You mean that?'

Carrie nodded. 'I really, really mean it.'

'I'm glad.' He smiled. Then as they stood there beneath the trees he reached out and touched the side of her face with his hand. 'You really are incredibly special to me, you know.'

'And you to me.'

It surprised her that she had said it. But now that the words were out she did not regret them.

She smiled at him. 'You were right. I was just angry and jealous.'

'I'm sorry you got hurt.' He slid his fingers through her hair, then let them curl softly round the back of her neck. 'You must learn to trust me more. It's quite safe, I promise you. The only woman in the world I want is you.'

Carrie could feel her heart thumping. The fiery touch of his fingers was turning her bones to powder as she stood there. And the way he was gazing at her made her feel as if she was drowning. She had to part her lips and gasp for air.

But before she could draw breath he was taking hold of her, very gently, then drawing her into his arms and kissing her.

'My angel.'

He held her close, his hands softly caressing her, his lips kissing her hair, her eyes, her mouth. And the warmth of him was engulfing her, and the scents of him, and the virile power of him. With a sigh Carrie wound her arms around his neck and pressed her lips against his face.

I could love this man, she thought, without surprise, just facing facts. This man could become the centre of my life.

He was looking down at her, eyes burning. 'I would suggest we go to my apartments...' He paused. 'But I know what that would lead to. I'd want you to stay the night. And maybe you're not ready for that yet— which I understand totally.' He kissed her softly on the mouth. 'So it's entirely up to you. If you'd rather, I'll take you home. After all, it's pretty late.'

The words hung in the air for only a moment. Carrie smiled at him and softly stroked his face with her fingertips. Then she shook her head and told him, 'I don't want to go home.'

There was no need to say more. Leone held her for
a moment, his breath shallow and fast as he kissed
her face lovingly. Then he took her by the hand and,
holding it very tight, led her in the moonlight back
to the palace.

Carrie had often dreamed what her first time would
be like. But it had never occurred to her that she would
lose her virginity in a vast Napoleonic bed beneath a
priceless Renaissance wall tapestry, her lover as
handsome as some Greek god, the whole scene bathed
in the soft, seductive glow of a magnificent pierced
brass Ottoman lamp.

But that was how it was. As magical as some fairy
tale and yet as real and immediate as the warm male
body that pressed against her, devouring her, intoxicating her, filling up all her senses. Nothing had ever
been so real or as magical before.

They had barely spoken a word on the way to his
apartments. Why talk when the touch of their bodies
said it all? And when they had finally reached his
rooms they had simply fallen into each other's arms,
each throbbing with helpless desire for the other.

And there were no foolish inhibitions, no holding
back at all, as they shed their clothes and fell down
on the bed, kissing and caressing each other with
frenzied hunger.

It seemed that no power on earth could stop what
was about to happen. The strength of their shared
passion was far too fierce.

And, as Carrie had known he would be, Leone was
a wonderful lover—gentle and wild and tender and
exciting. With masterful hands and lips, with slow

kisses and caresses, he unleashed the burgeoning whirlwind within her, till there was not an inch of her body that did not burn with excitement, nor a corner of her being that did not cry out for him.

Carrie did not tell him she was a virgin, and she knew it was unlikely that he would be able to tell. If she had told him he might have hesitated, or even drawn back, and she couldn't have borne to be denied him now.

As his hardness pressed against her and she took it in her hand she knew she had to feel that power deep within her, tearing her asunder, finally making her whole. Only his complete and total love could quench the ache in her loins.

At last, he drew himself on top of her and she shivered exquisitely, knowing that this was the moment she'd longed for. She would tell him the truth later: that there had been no other man before him. Now it did not matter. There were only the two of them in the universe anyway. For that was how it felt—as though the whole world had vanished, the only reality remaining what was happening between them.

The light from the big brass lamp that hung from the ceiling illuminated his features as he raised his face to look at her. And in that moment, as she seemed to slip into the endless pools that were his eyes, she knew with sudden clarity that she had been wrong a little earlier when she had thought that she could easily fall in love with him.

It had already happened.

She had fallen already.

I love him, she thought. What a glorious thing!

Her fingers laced in his hair, glorying in her discovery. It was all even more special now. Even more magical. And she shuddered as he gripped her flanks, his body poised to enter hers, his lips reaching for hers again, his breath hard in her ears.

I love you, I love you, I love you! she thought, kissing him back fiercely, pressing against him. My wonderful, wonderful, adorable Leone!

And a moment later she gasped with joy as their two bodies were joined.

It was much later, deep in the night, that, with a start, Carrie awoke. Where was she? Her heart was beating wildly inside her and a strange dread seemed to clutch at her throat.

She breathed slowly for a moment and anxiously reached out her hand, sighing with relief as it brushed against Leone. He was still here. She had not lost him. For that was the fear that had gripped her. To lose him now would have been too terrible to bear.

Though still deep in sleep, he had felt her hand brush against him and now he was reaching out to draw her to him, sighing with contentment as she curled against his back.

'My angel,' he murmured, as though in a dream.

Carrie wound her arms around him, pressing her face against his shoulders, as the wild beating in her chest began to slow at last. But though she tried to ignore it as she drifted back off to sleep she could still taste the bitter bile of dread in her throat.

CHAPTER EIGHT

LEONE was lying very still, propped up on one elbow, gazing at the most beautiful sight his eyes had ever seen. Carrie. Sleeping in the bed beside him. My angel, he thought with a sense of joy and wonder. And it seemed to him that he had never felt so happy in his life.

It was morning and the sun was filtering through the shutters, bathing the room in a rosy golden light. Down below, he could hear the swish of the sprinklers in the garden, and the occasional scurry of footsteps out in the corridor beyond the bedroom reminded him that the palace was getting ready for the day. But for once he was in no hurry to get up and get started. He would gladly have lain there and gazed at her all day.

It was funny, he was thinking, how things could happen. In the beginning, all she had really been was a pretty girl who had caught his eye and whom he had thought it would be fun to flirt with for a while—though, even in the beginning, there had been something special about her. But he had never suspected that he'd end up feeling like this.

He sighed, his blue eyes thoughtful. The things he was feeling were all new to him. No girl he had ever known had ever affected him this way. Sometimes he wondered if it could possibly last, but then all that happened was that it simply grew stronger. And little by little it seemed to be taking over his life. Which worried him a little. Sometimes worried him a lot. He wasn't sure if he was ready for this sort of thing.

She was stirring now. Lazily, her eyelids fluttered. She sighed a sleepy sigh. And then, suddenly, she was looking at him.

'*Buongiorno.*' Leone leaned over and kissed her. 'Hi,' he told her. 'Welcome to the world.'

'Good morning.' Carrie stretched. 'Have I slept terribly late?' She smiled at him. 'How long have you been lying there watching me?'

'A while. Maybe half an hour. You looked like an angel. But then you always do. My very favourite angel.'

Carrie laughed. 'You're crazy.' She reached up and touched his face. 'But I think I like you crazy. So I guess that's all right.'

'Only think?' He kissed her nose. 'You don't sound very sure.'

Not sure? Carrie looked at him. Oh, yes, she was sure. Opening her eyes just a moment ago to find him gazing down at her had caused her heart to melt with happiness. What a glorious thing to wake and find him here beside her. This wonderful man whom she loved with all her heart.

But she could not tell him that. Instead, she told him, teasing, 'First I have to find out just how crazy you are.'

'I see.' Leone smiled. 'Well, I'm crazy about you.'

As he said it he took her hand and held it against his lips, and as their eyes met and held and his lips caressed her fingers Carrie knew that, like her, he was thinking of last night. A shiver went through her. Last night had been special. A part of her that she hadn't even known existed had suddenly been awakened and given wings to take flight. And she knew that deep inside her she was changed forever.

She gazed into the blue eyes. And she had discovered that she loved him. That had been the most terrifying, most wonderful thing of all. And she longed to share it with him. But not yet. Not yet.

He kept telling her she was special and that he was crazy about her. Were these, she wondered, hoping, euphemisms for love? Her own feelings must remain locked away inside her until she knew for sure.

'So, now that you're awake, I suggest we have breakfast.' He continued to kiss her fingers as he spoke. 'We can have it here, if you like. I can phone down and order something.'

'That sounds nice.'

'So, what do you fancy?'

As he kissed her again, Carrie couldn't resist it. 'I don't know what I fancy.' She threw him a teasing look. 'Apart from you, of course, but maybe you're not on the menu.'

Then she giggled as, in response, he caught her in his arms and planted a big warm kiss on her lips. 'I'm always on the menu. Breakfast, lunch and dinner. And whenever you feel like a snack you just have to say the word.'

Carrie snuggled against him. 'You may be sorry you said that.' She let her hands travel lovingly over his hard body, caressing his chest, his shoulders, his back, feeling the muscles ripple sensuously beneath her fingers. 'I may turn out to have quite an appetite.'

'Is that a challenge, young lady?' Leone flipped her over, so that she was lying on her back and he was leaning over her. He held her there. 'It sounded rather like one to me.'

'So, what are you going to do about it?' Carrie laughed and kissed him. She felt quite wanton, and so happy that she could be so free with him. Then a thought suddenly struck her. As he kissed her shoulder she confided, 'You know, the first time I met you—well, it was the second time, actually, after I realised who you were—I was so totally confused that I wondered if I ought to curtsy to you. And now,' she added, playfully biting his ear, 'here I am lying naked in bed with you . . . Somehow I can't imagine curtsying to you any more!'

Leone teased her right back. 'That second time we met the last thing on my mind was whether you might curtsy to me or not. Frankly, I couldn't get over the length of your legs. I'd never seen such a fabulous pair in my life.'

As he said it he reached down and caressed her legs from shin to thigh-top, causing Carrie's insides to curl with helpless longing.

'And come to think of it,' he growled, bending to kiss her again, 'I wouldn't mind getting reacquainted with these legs.'

They eventually got round to ordering breakfast just before ten, after another unhurried bout of glorious lovemaking. And Leone was aware of Silvestro's diplomatically disguised smiles as he wheeled in the trolley with their coffee and croissants.

Carrie had insisted on hiding in the bathroom, in spite of Leone's assurances that that really wasn't necessary—Silvestro, like all his staff, was as discreet as the three wise monkeys—and, anyway, it was obvious that a woman had stayed the night and was still lurking around in a state of undress. There was a pile of underwear on one of the chairs, a discarded shoe lay beside the wardrobe and the unmistakable mingled scents of physical love filled the room.

And though, of course, Silvestro didn't say a word Leone knew he was surprised, for no woman had ever spent the night in his master's apartments before.

After breakfast, Leone gave Carrie a lift back to her flat.

'I really have to put in a few hours at the workshop,' he told her. 'But, if you're not doing anything else, why don't you come down about six? I can show you round and then we can go and have dinner.'

Carrie jumped at the chance, and it fitted in with her own schedule, which thankfully wasn't too heavy today. She wasn't sure if she could have coped with her usual demanding workday, for she was feeling decidedly unworkmanlike and dreamy! So, dead on six, she arrived at the impressive little workshop and spent a fascinating hour there, just watching what went on.

It was fascinating for lots of reasons. The cars were intriguing, for a start, and the whole place fairly buzzed with enthusiasm and expertise. Though she knew little about how cars worked—and even less about these Formula One jobs!—Carrie could appreciate the dedication and the sheer love of the men who worked on them. She felt privileged just to be around them.

But the most fascinating thing of all was just watching Leone, for at last she was beginning to understand a lot of things about him. The mystery of the true Leone was starting to unravel.

Amongst these men with whom he worked he was their peer and their equal. Not a count, not the brother of the ruler of the country, but a skilled engineer who was obviously respected and looked up to, and not for who he was but for the work he did.

He really belongs here, she thought as she watched him, full of admiration. And suddenly she felt even closer to him than ever. Here, in these surroundings, he was a working professional, just like her. How could she ever have thought of him as some kind of upper-class hooligan, as someone she could never be close to, almost from another universe?

Perhaps I only made myself believe that because I was afraid of my attraction to him and even more afraid of what it might turn into, she reflected. Probably what I was really doing was trying to protect myself.

Not that her strategy had worked, of course. She'd fallen in love with him anyway. In the event, there'd been no fighting it. It had been written in the stars.

'Are you ready? Shall we go?'

Suddenly he was beside her, kissing her, slipping an arm around her waist.

'Or would you rather stay on a while,' he teased, 'and learn some more about the cars?'

'It's you I've really been learning about over the past hour, not the cars.' As he locked up—for they were the last to leave the workshop—and they headed across the parking lot to where the little black sports car was waiting she confided, 'I think I finally know who Leone di Montecrespi is.'

He pulled the passenger door open for her. 'That sounds ominous. And here was me thinking I was making rather a good job of keeping you in the dark.'

Carrie pulled a face at him. He was teasing her again. 'You don't have to worry,' she told him. 'I rather like what I've found out.'

She expected him to smile or make some joke in response. But he did neither. Instead, his expression grew serious. Carrie found herself freezing, half in and half out of the car.

'What is it?' she asked. His strange look had made her anxious.

'Carrie, I—'

Still frowning, he laid a hand on her arm, and it was clear that there was a conflict going on inside him. Carrie felt a trickle of fear like a cold finger on her spine.

His eyes scanned her face, making her even more anxious. He said, 'There's something I ought to tell you.'

'Oh?'

Carrie swallowed. She felt suddenly cold and she was aware of a fearful pulse in her throat. Whatever was coming, she had the feeling she wasn't going to like it. Inwardly, she braced herself.

He was still watching her with that intent look, and the suspense was killing her. 'Carrie...' he said again. And as he paused she was dying. What on earth was he gearing up to say?

But then, abruptly, his expression altered. He smiled and shook his head and touched her cheek softly with his fingers. 'I'm crazy,' he told her. 'It's just that you bowl me over. There are a thousand things I feel I want to say to you, but what it all boils down to is I think you're terrific.'

Carrie almost fainted with relief. 'You're pretty terrific too,' she told him.

Then she was laughing as he swept her into his arms and kissed her. 'Come on, you wonderful girl. Let me take you out to dinner.'

The days and weeks that followed were the happiest Carrie had ever known.

If this is love, she decided, I definitely like it. For every second of every minute of every hour of every day was suddenly filed with the glow of sheer magic. It was as though the stars had dropped down from heaven and kissed her.

The two of them spent every possible moment together, eating, making love, laughing, talking—for they had endless things to say to one another.

Carrie told him all about her childhood in Colorado, about her wonderful parents and the grocery store they ran, and about her dear sister, Lauren, who was a teacher in Denver. And Leone, in turn, told her about his family and took her on the tour of the palace he'd once promised her, so she could admire the wonderful redecoration that his beloved mother had done. And bit by bit they got to know all about each other's life.

They laughed a lot, too. It was easy to laugh with Leone. In the past, at times, she had wondered if he was laughing at her, but now she realised she had been wrong about that. That wasn't his way. It was simply that he laughed easily. And that was one of the many, many things she loved about him.

But the nicest thing of all was simply being together, and often they would just lie with their arms round one another, not needing to say a word, just gazing at one another, joined by the precious bond that had grown between them.

And it was this feeling of being bound to him that Carrie found most intoxicating. He was a part of her now wherever she was, whatever she was doing, at whatever hour of the day or night. And she sensed that it was exactly the same for him too.

The word 'love' had never been spoken between them. Leone had told her he was mad about her, that she was the most wonderful girl alive, but he had never actually said those three important little words. And though at times, it must be said, Carrie longed to hear them—and to tell him in return that she loved him too—most of the time she didn't let it bother her. Love was just a word, she told herself. Not terribly important. What mattered was what they felt for each other in their hearts. And she knew without a doubt, for he proved it to her every day, that there was something very special in Leone's heart for her.

But then, too soon, the first crack in her happiness appeared.

It was another photograph on the front page of the morning paper that did it. Not that he had been snapped in the company of some half-naked girl this time. Anything but. The others with him in the photograph couldn't have been more soberly dressed. For it was a photograph that had been taken before the official dinner the previous evening in honour of some members of the British royal family who were currently visiting San Rinaldo.

And there was Leone, looking as Carrie had never seen him before, dressed in some braided and sashed formal uniform, standing with the Duke and Duchess, along with Lady Caterina and their distinguished royal guests. Carrie looked at the photograph and felt an icy coldness grip her heart. He didn't look like her Leone. He looked like someone she didn't know.

For a long time she stared at it, wishing she had never seen it. She had known about the dinner, of course. Leone had told her he'd be attending. She'd even picked up the newspaper expecting to see a photograph. But what she hadn't been expecting was its shocking effect on her. Suddenly, she was filled with a numbing, icy dread.

In an instant she was transported back to that first night she'd spent with him, when she'd suddenly awakened with the same sort of feeling—the sick, sobering certainty that sooner or later she would lose him. That this man who meant the world to her was destined not to be hers.

'Count Leone'. That was what was written in the caption beneath the picture. 'Brother of the Duke and heir to the throne of San Rinaldo'. And she knew all that, of course. Though somehow she had forgotten. She had forgotten the vast social gulf that divided them. She had fooled herself into believing that they were just two people in love—for that was how she thought of them, even though the words had never been spoken. But this photograph was spelling out to her that it could never be that simple.

The photograph had become a blur, but its message was still screaming at her. There could never be any future for them. It was out of the question. To kid herself otherwise was to live in never-never land. Their lives, their worlds, were too hopelessly far apart.

She closed her eyes in desolation. What a blinkered fool she'd been. She'd been kidding herself out of fear of facing the cruel truth.

And she still could not face it. She pushed these fears from her and, over the days that followed, determinedly forced herself to pretend that there was really nothing to be afraid of. But, alas, the rot had started and, after this initial jolt to her happiness, others began to follow in rapid succession.

They were having dinner one evening at one of their favourite restaurants when suddenly Leone grabbed her by the arm.

'Let's get out of here,' he told her, snatching her from her seat and hustling her through the door that led to the kitchen. 'We've been followed. That chap over there's a press photographer.'

He was right, and they only just managed to make their getaway—through the kitchen and out of the door at the back, followed by a quick sprint to where Leone's car was parked. And, though it felt quite exciting at the time, when Carrie thought about it later she realised that it had been rather unpleasant and such incidents could easily become a regular feature of their lives.

So far they'd been spared that simply because Leone was so careful. When they went out they only went to places where he was pretty sure they wouldn't be hassled, and he was always looking over his shoulder just in case they'd been followed.

'I don't mind being photographed when I'm on some official job,' he had told her once. 'I'm even prepared to put up with it when I'm on my own to some extent. I've got used to that by now and, like I told you once before, I tend to regard it as just part of the package.'

Then he had frowned at her and his tone was protective as he continued, 'But I'm damned if I'll stand for it when I'm with you. When I'm with you I want to be strictly private.'

Carrie had always been grateful for that. She had no desire whatsoever to live the sort of goldfish-in-a-bowl existence that tended to be thrust on the royal family. But after that incident at the restaurant, then another similar one a few days later, when a newsman suddenly jumped out at them while they were out walking on the beach, so that they had to do another rapid sprint to the car, she was beginning to seriously wonder if she would be allowed to escape for much longer.

Already there had been one or two mentions in a couple of newspapers of 'Count Leone's mysterious new companion', though no one as yet had identified who she was. And she dreaded that happening. Life, she feared, would become intolerable. She would never be able to regard it as 'just part of the package'.

Her spirits spiralled downwards. The relationship was doomed. She could never live that sort of life and Leone could never live any other. They were all wrong for one another. Her heart filled with misery. It was only a matter of time before the whole thing fell apart.

And as these feelings began to grow and establish themselves in her mind another dark feeling inevitably followed.

Leone must realise as well as she did that nothing could ever come of their romance. He'd probably realised it right from the start. More than likely that was why he'd never told her he loved her and why he never spoke about the future. He knew there could never be any future for them.

Her heart cracked as she thought these things. They were too painful to endure.

She said nothing to Leone. She was too afraid of tempting fate. But then, one evening, he seemed to confirm her worst fears.

They were having dinner at a favourite restaurant and both of them were in good spirits. They'd been chatting away as usual, Leone recounting his day at the workshop while Carrie filled him in on what she'd been up to.

Then suddenly she said, 'You know, I'm making incredible progress. I've finished all the work on the Montecrespi dinner service and there isn't even much left to do at the factory.' She laughed. 'I can hardly believe I've been so busy!'

'You're a hard-working girl.' There was admiration in his eyes. But then he frowned. 'So, how long do you reckon before you're finished?'

Carrie felt a tightening inside her. She tried not to think of that. Of leaving San Rinaldo and going back to New York. Of leaving Leone. The very thought destroyed her.

She said, glancing at her plate, afraid to look at him, 'I don't know. Two, maybe three weeks.'

'And then what?'

And then what? What exactly was he asking her? She was aware of a sudden nervous pulse in her throat.

Still not looking at him, she answered, 'After the book's finished? Well, there are one or two other things in the pipeline. My publisher seems quite keen on a book about—'

But that was as far as she got. He reached and took her hand. 'What I'm really asking, Carrie, is are you going to stay on in San Rinaldo? I want you to,' he added quickly. 'I don't want you to go back to the States.'

Carrie looked up at him then, her heart weak with love for him. She had longed to hear him say that he wanted her to stay on. But it wasn't enough. She needed more than that. For suddenly, more desperately than she'd ever felt it before, she was filled with the need to hear him say that he loved her. She held her breath and could not speak.

He was still holding her hand. 'There's no reason, after all, why you can't make San Rinaldo your base. You can work from here just as easily as you can work from New York.' He paused. 'What do you say?' Then suddenly he smiled. 'Actually, I don't care what you say. I won't let you go.'

Carrie's stomach was churning. She tried to smile back at him. But, deep inside, her heart was aching. It's not my work I'm worried about, it's *us*! she felt like shrieking. For if she stayed, what future did he envisage for the two of them? The question was choking her, but she did not dare ask it.

She said, her voice croaky, 'It's a big decision.'

'I know, but you're happy here.' He gave her hand a squeeze. 'We're good together, Carrie. Let's hang onto what we've got.'

Carrie's heart was throbbing. But what have we got? she felt like shouting. An affair, that's all it is, and that's clearly the way you want to keep it. She dropped her gaze away as pain lashed inside her. There was no way she could stay on for just an affair.

She said, sick with misery, 'I'll have to think about it.'

'OK. Think about it.' He reached with his free hand and tilted her chin, forcing her to look at him. 'I know it's a big decision.' He looked at her for a long time and the expression in the blue eyes was dark and persuasive. Then he smiled again, though still serious, and told her, 'I really meant it, you know. I won't let you go.'

Carrie returned home that evening in a state of turmoil. There could be no more hiding her head in the sand now. It was time she faced all the questions that were troubling her.

She stood before the big illuminated mirror in the bathroom and stared intently at her reflection. On the one hand she was afraid that if the relationship progressed she might not be able to handle some of the baggage that went with it. The paparazzi. The public scrutiny. She would find all that unbearable. She just wasn't cut out to be a countess.

But on the other hand she couldn't settle for being less than his wife. It just wasn't in her to accept the role of mistress. She felt a clench inside her. And it was starting to look as though that was the only role Leone had in mind for her. He certainly wasn't rushing to invite her to become his countess!

So it seemed as though the relationship was destined to go nowhere. But she loved him. Maybe it was hopeless, maybe it was all wrong, but she simply couldn't bear to lose him. She sank her head into her hands and tried to stifle her cold fear. She was a fool, but somehow she just had to keep on hoping.

And so she did. For a while. She even told him she might stay on—to which he predictably replied that he would give her no choice. But then came the final blow that wiped all that out.

She was in the waiting room of a local optician— who also happened to be a keen collector of Castello porcelain and with whom she had arranged to do an interview—and it was pure chance that she picked up that particular magazine, which was one of several in the pile that were in English. It was also pure chance— or was it really fate?—that she flicked the magazine open at that fatal page and saw the article that was to turn her heart into a wasteland.

'I'LL NEVER MARRY A COMMONER, COUNT LEONE TOLD ME.' That was the headline that screeched across the page. And attached to it was the story of one of Leone's ex-girlfriends, who'd been spurned because she wasn't good enough for him.

Carrie read the story from start to finish, her hands trembling, her poor heart turning to stone.

He told me he loved me. I thought he was serious. I thought we would marry. But then, when I pressed him, he admitted he would never marry me. I wasn't suitable to be his wife. I was only a commoner. He said he would only ever marry someone with a title.

The story ended with a sober warning. It claimed:

Any ordinary girl who gets mixed up with Count Leone is simply asking for heartbreak. He'll charm you and lead you on and make you fall in love with him—but don't be fooled. Really, he's just using you. To him you're nothing but a disposable plaything.

Somehow, Carrie managed to get through her interview. But once she was back home she collapsed in her room and gave way to a helpless storm of tears.

Well, one thing was quite clear. She'd be a fool to go on hoping now. What had happened to that girl was what would happen to her. Leone would never marry her. It was all just a cynical game to him. He had simply made a fool of her from start to finish.

She brushed the tears from her face and wondered bitterly if perhaps, after all, she ought to be pleased that he had never told her that he loved her. At least he had been honest about that. Well, he hadn't needed to lie, had he? She'd fallen into his arms like a ripe plum anyway.

The tears came again. Tears of anger and grief and a terrible, all-consuming black despair. There was no way she could stay now. She must return to the States. It was the only decent option open to her.

But he had said he would not let her go—for he wanted their affair to continue—and he'd be a hard man to fight. And there was the danger that she might weaken. But she must not. She must simply find a way to convince him. And preferably as soon as possible.

The solution cropped up, miraculously, just two days later. Carrie was having breakfast alone—she'd told Leone she was tired last night—when she received a phone call that turned out to be a gift from heaven.

It was from her old friend Bud, calling from New York.

'I'm coming to San Rinaldo in a few days,' he told her. 'I've got to stop off there on my way to a conference in London. I was rather hoping,' he told her, 'that we might be able to meet up.'

'Of course! I insist on it!'

Carrie would have been delighted to see him anyway. She'd known Bud for years and he was always fun to have around. But even as she was speaking to him a plan was brewing in her head. Having Bud around could provide the ideal solution.

By the time she laid down the phone her plan had taken firm shape and she knew now exactly how she must proceed. And she must do it. She clenched her fists. She must not lose this opportunity. For this plan of hers would work. She was absolutely sure of it.

She closed her eyes. She must be brave. She must allow nothing to divert her—even though, just at the thought of what lay ahead, she could feel the very life drain out of her.

Carrie decided to put her plan into action that evening. To put off would be fatal. If she waited, she might lose her nerve.

Not that she was exactly serene when Leone came to pick her up. Though she was struggling to hide it, inside she was a bag of nerves.

'Let's go to my place,' Leone suggested as she climbed into the car. Then, seeing her strained look, he frowned. 'Are you all right?'

'I'm just tired,' Carrie lied. She could scarcely bear to look at him. She knew it was probably false, just as their whole relationship was false, but that concerned look on his face was cutting her to the quick. You're a fool, she told herself. A weak, gullible fool. 'I'll be OK,' she told him, 'once I have something to eat.'

It was a totally wretched evening. Carrie ate, tasting nothing, as she floundered about trying to make trite conversation, waiting for a suitable moment to present itself so that she could plunge into the set speech she had been rehearsing in her head. And all the while she was aware of Leone's eyes on her face, piercing, probing, feigning concern.

It was after Silvestro had brought them coffee that she decided to take the plunge. Leone had told him he wouldn't be required any more, so she could do what she had to do without fear of interruption.

Her heart as heavy as a stone, she sat back stiffly in her seat. 'Leone, there's something I have to tell you.'

He did not look surprised. He too sat back a little and regarded her calmly across the table. 'In that case,' he said, 'you'd better get on and tell me. I've sensed there was something wrong all evening.'

So he had not been taken in by her pale attempts at subterfuge. Somehow, that made her task a little easier.

She took a deep breath. 'This isn't easy,' she began, 'but I've decided it's time I made a confession.'

'A confession?'

One straight black eyebrow had lifted. His eyes held hers. Expressionless. Unblinking.

'Yes, a confession, I'm afraid.'

The words were strangling her. I could stop here, she was thinking, feeling sudden panic at what she was doing. I could say it was just a joke. Pretend I was only teasing him.

But all the hurt and the anger in her answered swiftly, No! Where's your pride? they demanded. This guy's taken you for a ride!

So she forced herself to continue, clearing her throat again. 'I feel terrible about this. I know you're going to hate me...but I haven't been quite truthful with you, I'm afraid...'

Leone said nothing, just continued to look at her unblinkingly.

'You see, what I haven't told you...what I should have told you from the beginning...is that I already have a boyfriend over in the States. Bud's his name, though he's more than a boyfriend, really... I mean, we're virtually engaged to be married.' She licked her parched lips. 'And now I'm afraid I've been caught out. He phoned this morning to say he's coming over to visit me.'

As she stopped speaking, a silence as solid as a stone wall fell with a deafening crash between them. It was, Carrie would always remember, the worst moment of her life.

Then Leone said, 'You're right—you definitely should have told me. I'm rather astounded that you didn't.'

He sounded so cold that she could feel the blood freeze in her veins. She'd never thought she would ever hear him speak to her like that.

She said lamely, stiffly, 'It never came up.'

There was another long pause. The blue eyes narrowed as they watched her. As sharp as sabres. As hard as steel.

'Never came up?' He smiled a dark, humourless smile. 'I would say it came up every time we were together. Every time I kissed you. Every time we made love.'

'I mean you never asked me.'

'You're right—I never asked you. One expects to be told such things without having to ask.'

Yes, he hated her now. Carrie could hear it very clearly in every clipped and hostile syllable he spoke. He didn't mind playing with girls like her, but he didn't like being played with. Which was fine, she decided. Her plan had worked perfectly. There was no way he would try to make her stay now. In fact, she sensed that he couldn't wait for her to walk out the door.

She stared into her lap, rather wishing she could walk out now. She had achieved what she'd wanted, but she felt sick to her soul.

'I'm sorry I didn't tell you sooner,' she mumbled.

'Oh, don't apologise to me. The one you should apologise to is your fiancé.' For a moment he regarded her with undisguised distaste, then he straightened in his chair and glanced at his watch. 'In the circumstances, I would say that our original idea to wind this evening up early was a very good one indeed.'

He tossed down his napkin. 'Just as soon as you've finished your coffee, it'll be my pleasure to take you home.'

In fact, Leone did not escort her home personally. While she was getting her jacket he made a phone call, and when they got down to the courtyard a chauffeured limousine was waiting.

He pulled the door open for her and stood aside as she climbed in. 'Goodbye,' he told her tonelessly. And then he slammed the door behind her.

And Carrie didn't even have a chance to say her own goodbye before the car was sweeping round and heading for the gates, taking her away from the Palazzo Verde for ever.

CHAPTER NINE

IT WAS all nonsense, of course. A lie from start to finish. But it had served its purpose and that was all that mattered.

Or was it? Now that it was done, Carrie felt torn apart with horror, her heart gripped by a grief so fierce and so terrible that at times she felt she must surely die from it.

So this, she reflected numbly, was what it felt like to lose him. This sense of utter, total desolation. And she almost laughed out loud to remember how she'd worried that she might not want to share her life with him because of the lack of privacy. That seemed ludicrous now. All the paparazzi in the world were just a small inconvenience compared to the agony she felt now.

And the agony was compounded over the days that followed by a spine-chilling, steadily growing conviction that she'd just made the biggest mistake of her life. She should never have done it. She'd been far too hasty. For—who knew?—maybe that story in the magazine had been a lie. Maybe Leone had never said he would never marry a commoner. Maybe the girl had just invented that, out of spite and to make money.

No, she had ruined things for nothing. She became more and more convinced of it. She'd always felt that Leone loved her, even though he'd never said so.

161

Hadn't she sensed there was a special bond between them?

And the question of marriage? Well, it was early days for that yet. There'd been no need for her to get all anxious and paranoiac. She should have just been patient and let things take their course.

And one thing was for sure. Whatever happened— whether in the end he wanted to marry her or just to keep her as his mistress—nothing could be worse than being without him. She could cope with anything else, but not with that.

So, taking her courage in both hands, she picked up the phone and punched in Leone's private number at the palace. Somehow, she must undo this ghastly mistake.

'I want to speak to Count Leone,' she said firmly when his secretary answered.

'I'm afraid the Count is out at the moment. Can I take a message?' Pierre responded.

Carrie hesitated and then said, 'No. I'll phone back tomorrow. Tomorrow morning early, if that's all right?'

'I'm sure he'll be available then. Can I take your name, *signorina*?'

But already Carrie was saying goodbye and quickly breaking the connection. She didn't want to leave her name and alert him that she'd be calling. He might decide not to be there and she couldn't bear that. No, she must catch him by surprise and throw herself on his mercy. Tell him she'd been mad, crazy with confusion, and that the story she'd spun him had been an entire pack of lies. Forgive me, she would beg him. I love you. I love you.

But next morning, just as she was about to pick up the phone, she made the mistake of quickly glancing at the morning paper. And there on the front page were splashed two stories, adorned with photographs and blaring headlines, that caused her heart to turn to sawdust in her chest.

The first, the bigger one, was about Caterina. There was a photograph of her climbing into a car in tears, and below the photograph was a story about how the Duke had refused her permission to marry her lover. If she went ahead, according to the report, she would be cut off without a cent.

As Carrie read the story she almost wept for Caterina. Poor girl, she had been so in love, so happy. And now all that was gone because of her brother—about whom Carrie now swiftly revised her opinion. She had thought he seemed a fair man, but she had been seriously mistaken. He had forbidden his sister's marriage simply because her boyfriend was a commoner.

Carrie's heart had turned to a block of ice when she'd read that. Here she'd been trying to persuade herself that that magazine article, the one she'd read in the optician's waiting room, was probably just a pack of malicious lies, that Leone had never said he would never marry a commoner. But even if he hadn't, she realised now, it really made no difference anyway. What applied to Caterina would apply also to Leone. The Duke would never allow his brother to marry a commoner.

She smiled wryly and glanced down at the second picture on the front page. Not that Leone could be said to have marriage on his mind anyway. He was back to his old ways—if indeed he had ever left them—and, to prove it, here he was dancing the night away, cheek to cheek, with a rather stunning brunette.

Carrie laid down the paper with stiff, cold fingers. Well, that settled that, then. For one thing was quite clear—she wouldn't be making any phone calls now to the palace.

In fact, she did make one, for it seemed only decent to call Caterina and tell her how sorry she was about what had happened.

The conversation was brief, for Caterina was still very upset, though she was at pains to tell Carrie how much she appreciated her gesture.

'I'll phone you some time soon,' she said, 'once I'm feeling a bit better. Right now I'm hardly capable of putting two words together.'

Carrie was well acquainted with the feeling. These days, misery was her constant companion. It followed her like a black cloud wherever she went.

But at least Bud's arrival the following day cheered her up a bit.

She and Bud had known each other since college. They'd always been just friends—never any question of romance—and Carrie had always enjoyed his company enormously. A big, jovial man, he was always full of funny stories—and that was precisely what she needed now. Someone to lift her out of herself.

And their two days together were definitely a tonic, though Carrie discovered that even Bud's company couldn't lift her out of herself for very long.

At times, when they were together, she would briefly find herself forgetting about the aching misery in her heart. But at other times it was as though the very normality of Bud's company simply served to underline how hopeless she felt. It was as though she would never again be able to function normally. To be able to laugh and joke and feel light-hearted. It was just impossible to imagine the blackness of her soul ever lifting.

These feelings were at their worst on Bud's last evening. They had dinner at a restaurant—though Carrie ate very little and found herself barely contributing to the conversation. Then Bud walked her home, up the winding road beneath the trees, and it was just as they were coming around the final curve, at the point where the villa suddenly sprang into sight, that, surprising her, Bud took hold of her arm and said, 'I wish you'd tell me why you're so sad.'

The total unexpectedness of the kind gesture—for Carrie had told him nothing about her heartbreak—caught her by the throat and made the tears fly to her eyes. Unable to speak, she stared hard at the ground.

And neither she nor Bud noticed, as they walked the final few yards, the black sports car, hood up, parked on the other side of the road.

Bud and Carrie continued to walk in silence for a moment. Then Bud said, 'You know, sometimes it helps to talk.' And he gave her arm an encouraging little squeeze.

Carrie shook her head blindly. Her throat was raw and aching from the effort of trying to hold back the tears.

'Come on, hon. I can see it's nearly killing you.' There was real pain in his voice. 'I can't bear to see it.'

It was too much. In her frail state she could not bear such kindness. Carrie turned to look at him and found she could not speak. Then something inside her snapped. With a little cry of anguish she threw her arms around his neck.

And that was when, with a vicious squeal of tyres, the low black sports car shot away from the kerb as its driver stamped down hard on the gas. His face was rigid with fury. He should have known better, he was thinking. He should have realised he'd only be wasting his time.

For Leone had been waiting there at the kerbside for more than an hour after she had failed to answer his ring on the doorbell. It had been intuition that had brought him. But that intuition had been wrong.

For when he had got the message from Pierre a couple of days ago that a young lady sounding remarkably like Signorina Carrie had phoned him, refusing to give her name, but promising to ring back the following morning, Leone had dared to hope that a change of heart might be on the cards.

Maybe she'd broken off with her boyfriend. Maybe she'd had second thoughts. He'd waited for her to call again but, when no call had come, he had decided to go and confront her himself. For he had a strange feeling in his bones that things were not quite as she'd told him—that it wasn't over yet, that there was still a crumb of hope.

More fool me, he was thinking now as he drove like a maniac along the highway, heading for the Palazzo

Verde. He had seen with his own eyes that her romance was still thriving, and he felt bile on his lips as he saw again in his mind's eye that moment when she had thrown her arms around her lover's neck.

Well, I'm glad I saw it, he told himself. There could be no more doubts now. It was definitely over. Finished. Done.

He glared furiously at the road ahead, black flames leaping from his face. And of one thing, in his heart, he was absolutely certain. No matter what might happen, he wouldn't have her back now, even if she crawled to him naked over broken glass.

Bud flew off to London the following day.

Carrie saw him off at the airport knowing that she would miss him, though he had promised to call her from time to time and see how she was doing. For he had been distressed by her unhappiness and anxious to comfort her. He really was the kindest friend in all the world.

In the end, of course, Carrie had told him everything and he had listened with a wise, patient look on his face. And what had he told her? He had told her, 'Hang on in there. In life you never know how things are going to turn out, and in my experience love is a powerful force. So don't give up yet, hon. I reckon anything could happen.'

Carrie had reflected endlessly on this prognosis. Could he be right? she kept asking herself, over and over. Should she really go on hoping? Or would she simply be fooling herself?

If she and Leone got back together again, could there really be a future for them, in spite of the Duke's opposition? Or would he simply do to them what he had already done to Caterina?

And, of course, there was another small problem to consider. The small, crushing matter of the brunette in the photograph.

Carrie's mind spun round in circles, reaching no conclusion. At times, she dared to hope. At others, she despaired. The only thing that never changed, the thing that was constantly with her, was the misery that gnawed, without release, at her heart.

It was a couple of days later that, out of the blue, Caterina called, inviting Carrie to come round for tea.

'I'm feeling a bit more human now,' she said, 'and I'd love to see you.'

So Carrie ended up spending an enjoyable afternoon at the palace. Caterina was far from in high spirits— no more than was Carrie herself—but at least she hadn't lost her sense of humour and was trying hard to be philosophical about the situation. And, to Carrie's relief, Leone's name wasn't even mentioned, though Carrie did tell Caterina a bit about her pleasant couple of days with Bud.

When Carrie left, insisting that she could find her own way out, for Caterina had a pressing appointment in her office, she was feeling almost philosophical herself. Whatever happens, I'll survive, she was telling herself firmly as she made her way with quick strides along the corridor. But then she turned a corner and in her very next breath all her fine philosophy unravelled at her feet.

'Were you looking for me?'

Leone was standing before her and every muscle in her body had turned to water.

It was little more than a week since she'd last seen him, but suddenly it felt like for ever and she wondered, with a twist of anguish, how she had ever survived without him. He meant everything in the world to her. He was her reason for living. Just looking at him now made her soul weep with pleasure.

'Well, were you?'

He was dressed in a pair of light blue trousers, with a blue-striped shirt, sleeves rolled back to the elbows, that looked perfectly stunning with his tanned skin and jet-black hair. He was the most marvellous-looking creature she had ever seen in her life.

But there was no hint whatsoever of that smile she so loved. As he looked down at her there was a dark, impatient frown between his brows.

'I hope not,' he added brusquely. 'That would have been rather a waste of time.'

It took Carrie a moment to pull herself together. What was he saying? He'd been asking if she'd been looking for him. She shook her head hurriedly. 'No. I've been visiting your sister.'

'Then what are you doing here?' One dark eyebrow lifted. 'If your visit is over, why aren't you just leaving?'

'I am. I was.'

Carrie was suddenly acutely conscious of just how hard and hostile his tone was. In her confusion it hadn't quite registered until this moment. But it was very clear indeed that he was far from pleased to see her. In fact, he seemed angry that she should be here at all.

The realisation crushed her. He really does hate me, she thought miserably.

Leone continued to stand over her, eyes like barbed wire as he looked down at her. 'I repeat, in that case, what are you doing here?'

'I— What do you mean?' Suddenly confused, Carrie glanced round her. 'Surely this is the—?' Then she stopped and flushed to her hair roots. She was not where she'd thought she was. This was not the way out. Somehow, she'd strayed into Leone's private quarters.

Oh, Lord, she thought, I'm losing my marbles. What on earth could I have been thinking of?

Leone had his own theory about that. 'If you were coming to see me, as I said before, that would have been rather a waste of time. I can't think that you and I have anything to say to each other these days.'

'Perhaps not.'

The coldness in his eyes was chilling. Unable to bear it, Carrie dropped her gaze to the carpet. Though it wasn't true, she was thinking; there were some things she'd like to say to him, things that might thaw that ice-cold hate in him. Like that it had all been a lie that she had a boyfriend. That the only man she loved, or could ever love, was him.

She raised her eyes slowly to look into his face again. It was she who had made him hate her. And now she must take that hate away.

'Actually, I wasn't looking for you. I must have been dreaming and got lost.' She took a deep breath and frowned at him earnestly. 'But I'm glad I bumped into you. There are some things I'd like to sort out.'

'Sort out?' His tone was scathing. 'I think it's a little late for that. It seems to me you've already got things pretty well sorted out.'

'But I haven't. That's the point.'

'No?' His eyes swept over her, taking in the short white skirt she was wearing that revealed the tantalising length of her legs, the neat waistcoat top, the blonde hair brushed back from her face. 'You look as though you've got things very well sorted out to me. You look as though there isn't a hair out of place in your life.'

'That's not so.'

'You surprise me.'

'Leone.' She stepped towards him. 'There's something I have to tell you. It's about Bud. I . . .'

'Ah, yes. Bud.'

He had cut in sharply, and though he did not step back he managed nevertheless to give the impression of once more widening the gap between. Perhaps it was the look in his eyes, or the way he was standing, but there was a bottomless gulf a mile wide between them.

His eyes swept over her again, but this time scathingly. 'Now that he's gone, you must be missing him. He has gone, I presume, and that's the reason you're here to see me? Suddenly you find yourself at a loose end.'

'That's not the case. It's nothing like that.' Carrie felt deeply insulted at the very suggestion. Though it was her own fault that he thought that, after what she had told him. She insisted, 'Leone, it's nothing like that.'

But he wasn't listening. 'You don't like a cold bed, do you? You need a lover—any lover—to warm it up for you.' His eyes were as harsh as winter and full of contempt for her. 'Well, I'm terribly sorry but I'm not for hire this time. I'm afraid you'll have to find yourself another stud.'

It was as though he had slapped her. Carrie felt herself recoil from him. This was one insult she most definitely did not deserve!

'Where the devil's that coming from? How dare you speak to me like that? I demand that you apologise immediately!'

'Apologise?' He laughed brutally. 'That's the last thing I'll be doing. Still, I admire your gall in coming up here, just like that, dressed to the nines, touting your wares...'

'I'm not dressed to the nines! I'm dressed the way I always dress—'

But he cut in coarsely, eyes scanning her long legs, 'You know my weakness, so you came suitably rigged out. Well, the legs are gorgeous, as I've told you many times, but there are no takers this time. You'd better try someone else.'

'You're unspeakable!'

Carrie was almost choking with anger, but somehow she managed to force the words out. Her hands were clenched into fists. She wished she could punch him. Lay him out cold on the crimson carpet.

She glared at him. 'Your trouble is you think everyone's like you! You think everybody sleeps around like you do. A blonde one night, a brunette the next...

And what will it be tonight?' she demanded cuttingly. 'A redhead?'

He paused for only as long as it took to compose his stony features into a cruel and gloating smile. 'No, I'm having the brunette again. She rather appealed to me.' He fixed her with a look that was totally without pity. 'I take it you're referring to the one in the photograph the other day? She was rather special, wasn't she? With legs even longer than yours.'

Carrie couldn't help it. She felt the blood drain from her face and suddenly her skin had grown as cold as marble. Something stuttered inside her. She felt a huge grief well up. So, it was true, after all. The very thing she had feared most.

She said thinly, only just managing to force the words between her lips, for the muscles had gone quite numb and stiff, 'Congratulations. I hope you enjoy her.'

'Oh, I shall, don't worry.'

Leone had noticed her pallor, but though he gained no satisfaction from it it did not move him either. She was mistaken if she thought she could play these games with him. Gravely mistaken. He would teach her a lesson.

He continued as she remained silent, 'And I wish you enjoyment with Bud—or whoever you choose to fill in for him until you see him again.'

'No one will be filling in.'

'You'll be seeing him again soon, then?'

'I expect I shall. After all, I'll be going home soon.'

Though not nearly soon enough, she was thinking, dully. For suddenly she was filled with a near-frantic desire to be gone from this place at the earliest possible opportunity. And not just gone from the palace, which she longed to flee from right this minute, but gone from the entire state of San Rinaldo, which she was suddenly realising could only bring her pain now. If she was to save what little remained of her precious sanity, she must pack her bags and get out of here, fast.

She began to step away. For a start, she would end this conversation. But then Leone said, 'So, when are you planning to leave? I suppose you've got about another week here?'

That would have been right according to her earlier calculations, but even as she looked at him Carrie found herself revising that.

But she revealed nothing to him. 'I expect so,' she answered. Then she began to move away again. 'And now I really have to go.'

Leone did not try to stop her. He just stood where he was and watched her as she turned round and headed back the way she'd come. But if she'd glanced across her shoulder Carrie might have been surprised at the fiercely intense expression in his eyes. It wasn't malice. It wasn't anger. It was something closer to regret. And it followed her till she'd turned the corner and disappeared from sight.

But Carrie was aware of none of that. Her mind was focused on something else now. For she was trying to work out just how long it would actually take her to finish the work she still had to do here and get on a plane back to America and sanity. And by the time she'd reached the courtyard where a palace limousine

was waiting for her she'd come to a highly satis-
factory conclusion.

If she worked day and night, virtually every hour
that God sent, she could wrap everything up within
seventy-two hours.

She climbed into the back of the limo and sat back
with a grateful sigh. Only three more days of pur-
gatory to go.

CHAPTER TEN

'DR LAMBERTI, I want to thank you for all the help you've given me. I don't know what I would have done without you.'

'The pleasure has been all mine, Signorina Carrie.' Dr Lamberti beamed and shook her hand warmly. 'And remember, if you're ever back in San Rinaldo you must drop in at the factory and pay me a visit.'

'Oh, don't worry, I would. That's one thing you can count on.'

Carrie said it sincerely, for if she ever was back in San Rinaldo the charming manager of the Castello factory was one person she would definitely want to see again. But she would never be back, of course. That was absolutely certain. When she flew out of here tomorrow it would be goodbye for ever.

Back in her little office Carrie finished packing up her things. She had said all her goodbyes now and it had been dreadfully emotional, for she had met so many wonderful people during her stay here. She knew she would remember them as long as she lived.

She'd called Caterina last night at the palace to say goodbye and had felt a little guilty at her friend's surprise at her sudden departure.

'I thought you'd be here for a while yet. I was hoping to see you again. What a pity. And I can't even see you tomorrow. I have to go to Vienna for a couple of days.'

'I'm sorry, Caterina. It's just the way things happened. I have to leave a little earlier than I'd anticipated ...' Carrie had let her voice trail off. She could scarcely go into details. 'But I'll keep in touch, and I hope everything works out well for you. And—who knows?—maybe our paths will cross again.'

It would be lovely if they did, she thought to herself now as she dropped the last few bits and pieces into her briefcase, snapped the lock shut and glanced at her watch. She had grown fond of Caterina and she'd sensed that they might have become good friends. But the sad fact was that they would probably never meet again.

She picked up her briefcase and headed for the door. The car Dr Lamberti had laid on to take her home would be waiting for her down at the main door. And as she headed for the ground floor, down the elegant marble staircase, she smiled a wry little smile to herself. At least she would be able to keep an interested eye on what was happening in Caterina's life, through the reports that would be published in all the newspapers and magazines, even though Caterina would know nothing about hers.

And that was when it suddenly struck her that the fairy tale really was over. Her glamorous association with the Montecrespi family finally had come to an end. She would miss it all a little, for it had been an exciting time. The trips to the palace in the black limousine. Meeting the Duke. Making friends with Caterina. It had definitely been something out of the ordinary and it had provided her with lots of happy memories to look back on.

She preferred not to think about the darker side of the coin—about Leone and her love for him and how it had all come to nothing. That wound was still too raw to bear even the most delicate probing. She was just glad to be going, to be leaving him behind her. Perhaps once she had put some distance between them her heart might finally start to heal.

The car carried her towards home, up the winding, tree-lined road, and she sat forward as they turned the bend and the villa came into view. A moment later, they were drawing up outside.

'Thank you,' she told the driver, handing him a generous tip, for he had done her this service several times before.

Then, without a backward glance, she was hurrying through the gates and up the stairs to her flat for the very last time.

Carrie woke up with a violent ringing in her ears.

Still struggling from sleep, she reached out with a groan to switch off the alarm on the bedside table. What misery! Was it really time to get up already? It felt as though she'd only just fallen asleep!

And she had! As her eyes focused with difficulty on the clock face she could see that it was only twenty to one. But it couldn't be that. Perhaps the clock had stopped? But it couldn't have stopped. If it had, it wouldn't be ringing!

She frowned for a moment in total confusion, then belatedly her brain slipped into gear. It *was* twenty to one and it wasn't the alarm that was ringing. That shrill, persistent racket in her ears was the doorbell!

Carrie pulled herself upright. What the devil was going on? Was the house on fire? Was somebody ill? Suddenly a little anxious, she jumped out of bed.

The bell was still ringing. It must be Signora Rossi, she decided, not bothering to pull on her dressing gown as she headed for the door. Poor woman. Whatever the problem was she sounded quite frantic!

Pushing back her tousled hair, she reached for the doorknob. 'Signora Rossi, what on earth's the matt—?'

The final syllable of the word hung unspoken in the air, for suddenly Carrie was blinking in disbelief.

It wasn't Signora Rossi on the doorstep.

It was Leone.

'I'd forgotten how soundly you sleep. I've been leaning on that bell for at least ten minutes.'

And though he smiled as he said it the smile never reached his eyes. Not for one moment did they lose their dark, troubled look.

But Carrie didn't notice that. She was too shocked to notice anything. For at the sight of him her poor heart had done a somersault in her chest as a shaft of mingled pain and pleasure shot through her. She'd been quite certain that she would never set eyes on him again and she realised now just how terrible that would have been. Though seeing him, in truth, was almost as terrible. To look at him was to feel the full weight of her loss.

She struggled to push back the pain as she looked into his face. 'What are you doing here?' Her tone was flat and accusing. 'Do you have any idea what time it is?'

Had he been out at some nightclub with his friends? she was wondering, eyeing the immaculate dark blue suit he was wearing. And had he decided, just for a bit of sport, to come and wake her up? Perhaps there was some woman waiting for him outside in his car?

Could it be that he had come here in order to humiliate her? Remembering what had passed between them last time, all these things seemed quite possible.

'Yes, I know what time it is, but I have to speak to you.' As he made this announcement Leone was standing squarely in the doorway as though not even a brigade of Guards would shift him. He added, narrowing his eyes at her, 'Caterina tells me you're leaving tomorrow.'

'Yes, I am.'

'That's rather sudden.'

'I've finished my work here.' She tilted her chin at him. 'And I have nothing to stay for.'

'No, I don't suppose you do.'

His eyes swept over her for a moment, making Carrie suddenly very conscious that she was wearing only a flimsy nightslip. In order to conceal herself a little—which she knew was pretty silly, for he had seen all this and more on plenty of occasions!—she began to edge the door shut just a little.

But instantly Leone was reaching out to stop her. 'I'm sorry, but I must insist,' he said, pushing the door open again. 'You and I have got to talk.'

'What about?' All at once her heart was clattering. 'As you said the other day, we have nothing to talk about.'

What did he want? she was wondering, her hand still on the door. Why was he being so insistent? And she felt totally torn, one terrified part of her wanting to demand that he leave immediately, for what could he have to say to her that she would want to hear? All he was likely to offer her were more insults and more pain.

But still she hesitated, a tiny spark of hope flickering. She was mad, of course, but she could not send him away.

So, when he insisted, 'Yes, we do. And we must talk now,' she smothered her terror and answered, 'You'd better come in.'

As he stepped into the hall Carrie quickly switched on the sitting-room light. 'Wait in there,' she told him before darting into her bedroom to retrieve her cotton dressing gown from where it lay over the wicker chair. It wasn't much of a protection, but she might feel a little less vulnerable with it on!

But when she emerged, tying the belt, she felt as vulnerable as ever as she caught sight of him in the sitting room, impatiently pacing the floor. He looked troubled, edgy, a tiger pacing its cage. And I'm the one he's going to pounce on and devour, she thought bleakly.

And it seemed she was right. As she stepped through the doorway he swung round abruptly to confront her with a snarl. 'Why did you tell me that Bud was your boyfriend?'

'And who says he isn't?'

Carrie was taken by surprise. What on earth had prompted him to ask questions about Bud? And something else had surprised her, for in the brightly lit sitting room she could see that he wasn't looking quite as immaculate as she'd first thought. The dark blue suit was a little crumpled, his shirt undone at the collar, and she could see now that dark, troubled look in his eyes.

She felt a sudden flash of sharp, unfocused anxiety. She frowned at him. 'What have you been up to? Why are you here?'

'What have I been up to?' He frowned back at her as he answered. 'I had an official dinner at the palace, then I drove Caterina to the airport.' He paused and the furrow between his brows grew deeper. 'Which brings me to the answer to your question... It was Caterina who told me that Bud isn't your boyfriend.'

Carrie said nothing, just stared at him mutinously. Why should she admit that Bud wasn't a boyfriend when he took such pleasure in flaunting his girl-friends in her face?

He was continuing, 'It came out completely by chance. She just happened to mention, as we were driving to the airport, that you were flying back to New York tomorrow. I made some cutting comment about you going back to see Bud, your lover, and she laughed and told me I'd got it all wrong, that Bud was nothing more than a friend.'

He took a step towards her, his expression men-acing, as though he might take hold of her and shake the truth out of her. The blue eyes glinted. 'Well?' he demanded.

'Well, maybe she's right. And maybe she isn't.'

Carrie wanted to step away, but couldn't quite bring herself to do so. The scent of him was in her nostrils. Intoxicating. Making her heart weep. She wanted to grab him and kiss him, and equally she wanted to hit him. Why did he have to torture her like this?

She let out a gasp of frustration. 'What's it to you?'

'What's it to me?' The blue eyes pierced her. Then, before she could stop him, he had grabbed her by the shoulders, his fingers like vices, digging into her flesh. 'I thought we had something going. Something special. And then you come and tell me you already have a boyfriend.' He gave her a sharp shake. 'Well, is it true or not?'

' "Something special!" And what's that supposed to mean?' Suddenly, something snapped inside Carrie, and as anger filled her she tore herself free of him. 'How can you talk about "something special" when you've been bedding that brunette? And not just bedding her, boasting about it to me as well!'

She barged on, feeling her outrage carry her along like a floodtide. 'But I knew what you were like. I should never have had anything to do with you. Men like you don't change. It's like a sickness in you.' As all her misery welled up, her voice caught on a sob. 'All I ever was to you was just another notch in your belt!'

'No, you were never that.'

He was very still as he looked down at her, as though he wanted to take hold of her but did not quite dare.

'When I first saw you,' he continued, 'I confess the attraction was largely physical, but once I got to know you it soon became much more than that...'

And now, at last, he did reach out and touch her. He laid a hand, as soft as thistledown, against her arm. The blue eyes poured over her.

'Carrie, I love you.'

At last, he had said it. But Carrie was close to weeping. She looked back at him in misery. 'How can I believe that?'

'For a start, by facing the fact that I'm not what you say I am. I'm not the kind of man you're talking about at all.' He frowned. 'I thought you knew me well enough by now to know that.'

'I thought I did too, but I don't any more.' Carrie's eyes were so blurry, she couldn't see a thing.

'Then you're crazy.' His hand was closing round her arm, holding her there, firmly but so gently. 'There was never any brunette, just like there was never any blonde. She was just the wife of someone I was required to dance with at some stupid reception. If you'd read the report that went with the picture you'd have discovered that for yourself.' He frowned. 'Dear Carrie. Why can't you trust me?'

Could that possibly be true? Carrie's heart squeezed with hope. For he was right; she hadn't even looked at the report.

Then she remembered. 'But you told me yourself you were spending the night with her!'

'A lie.' The blue eyes frowned. 'A stupid lie, Carrie. Partly because I was angry that you could accuse me of being unfaithful, and partly because I was still angry about you and Bud.' His gaze raked her face. 'But you still haven't answered my question. Is it true what Caterina told me—that Bud's only a friend?'

Carrie was catching her breath. Had the brunette really been a lie? Relief jolted through her. It seemed that she had.

She reached up and laid her hand against the lapel of his jacket, then let her fingers slide upwards to caress his face softly. 'Bud is only a friend. There's no other man in my life but you.'

Then she smiled a nervous smile. 'You said something a moment ago...but I'm not sure if I heard right. I really wish you'd say it again.'

Leone bent to kiss her face. 'You heard right. I love you. I should have told you a long time ago.'

'And I love you.'

At last, she could tell him. And saying it was almost as sweet as hearing it. As he took hold of her and held her tightly and kissed her, with a look of such relief and joy on his features, she had never felt so completely happy in her life.

Then he drew back and frowned at her, though still holding her close to him. 'So why did you lie to me? Why that story about Bud?'

Carrie explained as best she could, telling him quite candidly about her fears that they were too different, that there could never be any future for them. And she told him, too, about the article she had read in the magazine.

'It said that girls like me were only playthings in your book. I was devastated when I read that. I couldn't bear to be your plaything.'

'My plaything?' He frowned at her. 'Let me tell you something. First of all, from start to finish, that article was a libellous invention. I refuse to sue, so some people take advantage. They'll say anything as long as the cheque's big enough.

'Second, I never treat women as playthings—and certainly not the woman I've been looking for all my life. For that's what you are, you know.' He pulled a gently self-mocking face. 'I confess it scared me a little at first that I'd actually found you. I wondered if I was ready for the ultimate commitment.' Then he bent to kiss her face. 'But I love you, Carrie, and I just couldn't face a future without you.'

Carrie looked at him, heart throbbing. What was he saying? He'd said 'the ultimate commitment'. Was he talking about marriage?

Scarcely daring to breathe, she said, 'But what about your brother? I mean . . . after what happened with Caterina . . .'

Leone frowned for a moment as though he didn't understand. Then he smiled and told her, 'Don't worry about my brother. Damiano won't stand in our way. He has a very high opinion of you.' Then he shook his head at her. 'But even if he didn't I can assure you it wouldn't make a jot of difference.' The blue eyes flashed. 'Nothing in the world's going to stop me from marrying you.'

Carrie's heart had grown quite still. He had said it. She hadn't dreamed it. But still she had to put to him, 'How can you be so sure? He stopped your sister from marrying a commoner.'

'He stopped my sister from marrying a scoundrel. The fact that the guy's a commoner had nothing to do with it—though Caterina, for the moment, refuses to believe that.'

He stopped short and shook his head. 'But why are we talking about my sister? It seems to me we have far more important things to talk about.' He kissed Carrie's face. 'I was just saying, as I recall, that nothing in the world's going to stop me from marrying you . . .'

A flash of humour touched his eyes. 'But, before we go any further, I promised myself I was going to do this thing properly . . .'

And there, in the middle of Carrie's living-room carpet, he got down on one knee and proposed to her formally in the manner of his aristocratic European ancestors.

'I love you,' he told her. And his expression was sober now, the blue eyes dark and intense as he looked at her. 'Will you do me the honour of becoming my wife?'

Carrie felt quite overcome. She looked into his face, loving him with every inch and fibre of her being.

'Oh, yes,' she said, blinking back the tears that stung her eyes. 'I should love nothing more in all the world than to be your wife.'

And, as he let out a whoop of joy, she flung her arms around his neck, then they were laughing and kissing and rolling to the ground in what was really a most unaristocratic manner.

'Shall we make love?' Leone murmured.

'Oh, yes,' Carrie answered.

So he picked her up, gave her a huge warm kiss, then, without further ado, carried her through to the bedroom.

Carrie and Leone were married two months later beneath the gentle gaze of their favourite angel in the private chapel at the Palazzo Verde.

Both of them had wanted the ceremony to be as private as possible. 'Let's start out,' Leone had said, 'as we mean to continue.' Though, of course, they had done their bit at the time of their engagement, posing for the world's press, arms around each other, to show off Carrie's magnificent diamond ring—and, after the wedding ceremony was over, they would ride in an open carriage through the packed, cheering streets of Rino, the capital. But at the ceremony itself there were only family and close friends.

Carrie's parents and sister, Lauren, had flown over from the States—along with a dozen or so of Carrie's best friends, including, of course, Bud and Louise— and it was the proudest moment of Mrs Dunn's life as she watched her elder daughter, escorted by her father and looking a vision in her dress of white satin, walk to the altar where her bridegroom stood waiting.

'My daughter, a countess!' she sobbed into her hankie. 'I can't believe it. It's just like a fairy tale!'

'A countess, and a happy one,' Bud amended at her elbow. For he had never seen Carrie sparkle quite so brilliantly. The light in her eyes positively put to shame the glitter of the magnificent tiara on her head.

Everyone had noticed, not least Damiano and Sofia, now the parents of a healthy six-week-old son. And as Sofia watched her new sister-in-law she couldn't help envying her her happiness and hoping that this marriage might work out better than her own. Her own, she sometimes thought, must be the un-happiest in the world.

Wrapped in her own thoughts, too, was Caterina, as she watched her friend Carrie exchange vows with her dear brother.

I wish them joy, she was thinking, though I'll never follow in their footsteps. I'll never marry now. Love and romance are not for me. And as she blinked back the bad memories she cast a black look at Damiano. She would never forgive him for what he had done.

Then she pushed these thoughts away and turned her attention back to the happy couple. This was Leone and Carrie's day, and she smiled as she watched them. Surely there had never been two people who were so right for each other?

It was a simple ceremony, but a deeply moving one—particularly for the couple who stood at the altar, the tall man in the dark morning suit and the beautiful blonde girl in lace and satin, the two of them locked in a magical halo of love. And though Carrie felt at times as though she was floating in a dream she would remember every detail of this precious day for ever.

As Leone slipped the plain gold wedding band onto her finger she looked into his eyes, her love overflowing. Till death us do part, she thought, and felt her heart wobble. They were one now. For ever. Their happiness was complete.

At last the ceremony was over and the organ was playing and they were walking back down the aisle together. Then they were stepping out of the ancient chapel into bright November sunshine and heading for the horse-drawn carriage that was waiting.

And as Carrie was about to climb in she almost forgot until Leone reminded her, 'You've got to throw your bouquet.' And, laughing, she tossed it into the crowd.

She didn't notice that it was a shocked Caterina who had caught it as she took Leone's hand and climbed up into the carriage, dizzy with joy, glowing with happiness, still half-stunned by the fact that she really was married now to the most wonderful, most exciting man in the whole world.

Then Leone was climbing in beside her and taking her hand and the carriage was setting off, carrying them away, with a clip-clip-clop against the ancient cobblestones, to begin the first chapter of a wonderful new life.

*   *   *   *   *

Look out for Caterina's story next month in
THE LADY'S MAN!

GET 4 BOOKS
AND A MYSTERY GIFT

Return this coupon and we'll send you 4 Mills & Boon Romances and a mystery gift absolutely FREE! We'll even pay the postage and packing for you.

We're making you this offer to introduce you to the benefits of Reader Service: FREE home delivery of brand-new Mills & Boon Romances, at least a month before they are available in the shops, FREE gifts and a monthly Newsletter packed with information.

Accepting these FREE books and gift places you under no obligation to buy, you may cancel at any time, even after receiving just your free shipment. Simply complete the coupon below and send it to:

MILLS & BOON READER SERVICE, FREEPOST, CROYDON, SURREY, CR9 3WZ.

No stamp needed

Yes, please send me 4 free Mills & Boon Romances and a mystery gift. I understand that unless you hear from me, I will receive 6 superb new titles every month for just £2.10* each postage and packing free. I am under no obligation to purchase any books and I may cancel or suspend my subscription at any time, but the free books and gifts will be mine to keep in any case. (I am over 18 years of age)

1EP6R

Ms/Mrs/Miss/Mr _____

Address _____

_____

_____ Postcode _____

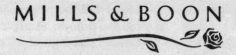

MILLS & BOON

Next Month's Romances

Each month you can choose from a wide variety of romance with Mills & Boon. Below are the new titles to look out for next month.